THE LION OF COMARRE

&

AGAINST THE FALL
OF NIGHT

ARTHUR C. CLARKE

THE LION OF COMARRE

&

AGAINST THE FALL OF NIGHT

HARCOURT, BRACE & WORLD, INC., NEW YORK

To Johnnie

INTRODUCTION

Although I remember very little about the young man who wrote *Against the Fall of Night,* I still know exactly how it all began. The opening scene flashed mysteriously into my mind, and was pinned down on paper, around 1935. It was an isolated incident, unrelated to any plot I had been trying to develop. Not for several more years did I start to expand it into a novel.

Between 1937 and 1946, at least five versions, of ever-increasing length, were developed. Those friends who were forced to read the successive drafts will smile ruefully at the news, in Sam Moskowitz's biographical study *Seekers of Tomorrow,* that I worked on the manuscript "secretly."

But Moskowitz quite correctly identifies the novel's major influences, of which the most important was William Olaf Stapledon's tremendous saga of future history, *Last and First Men.* I came across this volume in the public library of my birthplace, Minehead, soon after its first appearance in 1930. With its multimillion-year vistas, and its roll call of great but doomed civilizations, the book produced an overwhelming impact upon me. I can still remember patiently copying Stapledon's "Time Scales"— up to the last one, where "Planets Formed" and "End of Man" lie only a fraction of an inch on either side of the moment marked "Today."

A little later, "Don A. Stuart" (John W. Campbell) made a similar impact with his short story "Twilight," in *Astounding Stories,* November, 1934. But not all the ingredients were literary: at least one was musical (Debussy's *L'Après-midi*). And, undoubtedly, much of the emotional basis came from my transplantation from the country (Somerset) to the city (London), when I joined the British Civil Service in 1936. The conflict between a pastoral and an urban way of life has haunted me ever since; I could hardly have imagined that, thirty years later, I should resolve it by the drastic expedient of commuting around the world every few months, from Ceylon to New York.

By the end of World War II I had sold a number of short stories, and this encouraged me to complete *Against the Fall of Night* for publication. To my disappointment John Campbell (one of its godparents) turned it down, though with his usual long and helpful letter of constructive criticism. His main complaint was that it was too downbeat—though nothing could have been more downbeat than his own "Twilight" and its successor, "Night." I incorporated some of his suggestions, and tried my luck with *Astounding Stories* again—but John remained unsatisfied. As a result, the tale finally appeared in the November, 1948, *Startling Stories*, which infuriated me by giving it a completely misleading, sexy cover. It took real ingenuity to find any sex in the story line, but *Startling's* cover artist did his horrid best. Martin Greenberg's Gnome Press published the novel in hard cover a few years later (1953); this edition has long been out of print.

Despite all the effort I had put into the various drafts, the theme of the eternal city at world's end continued to obsess me. I felt that there was much more to be said on the subject; also, I had learned a good deal more about science—and writing—since the story was first conceived. After several full-length novels had been published, I returned again to Diaspar (pronounced, incidentally, Dyaspar).

The opportunity came during the long sea voyage from

England to Australia when I joined forces with Mike Wilson and set off on an underwater expedition to the Great Barrier Reef (see *The Coast of Coral*). The much longer and drastically revised novel, *The City and the Stars*, was completed in Queensland between excursions to the Reef and the Torres Strait pearling grounds. It was published by Harcourt, Brace & World in 1956, and has remained in print ever since.

At the time, I assumed that the new version would completely replace the older novel, but *Against the Fall of Night* showed no tendency to fade away; indeed, to my slight chagrin, some readers preferred it to its successor, and it has now been reissued several times in paperback (Pyramid Books). One day I would like to conduct a poll to discover which is the more popular version; I have long ago given up trying to decide which is the better one.

The search for a title took almost as long as the writing of the book. I found it at last in a poem of A. E. Housman's, which also inspired the short story "Transience":

> What shall I do or write
> Against the fall of night?

I have taken the opportunity presented by this volume to print another adventure which has never before appeared in book form. "The Lion of Comarre" was written at the same time, and is imbued with much the same emotions, as the longer work. Its only prior publication was in *Thrilling Wonder Stories* for August, 1949.

Though they are set eons apart in time, the two stories have much in common. Both involve a search, or quest, for unknown and mysterious goals. In each case, the *real* objectives are wonder and magic, rather than any material gain. And in each case, the hero is a young man dissatisfied with his environment.

There are many such today, with good reason. To them
I dedicate these words, written before they were born.

ARTHUR C. CLARKE

New York City
October 1967

The Lion of Comarre

1 ◄► REVOLT

Toward the close of the twenty-sixth century, the great tide of Science had at last begun to ebb. The long series of inventions that had shaped and molded the world for nearly a thousand years was coming to its end. Everything had been discovered. One by one, all the great dreams of the past had become reality.

Civilization was completely mechanized—yet machinery had almost vanished. Hidden in the walls of the cities or buried far underground, the perfect machines bore the burden of the world. Silently, unobtrusively, the robots attended to their masters' needs, doing their work so well that their presence seemed as natural as the dawn.

There was still much to learn in the realm of pure science, and the astronomers, now that they were no longer bound to Earth, had work enough for a thousand years to come. But the physical sciences and the arts they nourished had ceased to be the chief preoccupation of the race. By the year 2600 the finest human minds were no longer to be found in the laboratories.

The men whose names meant most to the world were the artists and philosophers, the lawgivers and statesmen. The engineers and the great inventors belonged to the past. Like the men who had once ministered to long-vanished diseases, they had done their work so well that they were no longer required.

Five hundred years were to pass before the pendulum swung back again.

▼

The view from the studio was breath-taking, for the long, curving room was over two miles from the base of

Central Tower. The five other giant buildings of the city clustered below, their metal walls gleaming with all the colors of the spectrum as they caught the rays of the morning sun. Lower still, the checkerboard fields of the automatic farms stretched away until they were lost in the mists of the horizon. But for once, the beauty of the scene was wasted on Richard Peyton II as he paced angrily among the great blocks of synthetic marble that were the raw materials of his art.

The huge, gorgeously colored masses of artificial rock completely dominated the studio. Most of them were roughly hewn cubes, but some were beginning to assume the shapes of animals, human beings, and abstract solids that no geometrician would have dared to give a name. Sitting awkwardly on a ten-ton block of diamond—the largest ever synthesized—the artist's son was regarding his famous parent with an unfriendly expression.

"I don't think I'd mind so much," Richard Peyton II remarked peevishly, "if you were content to do nothing, so long as you did it gracefully. Certain people excel at that, and on the whole they make the world more interesting. But why you should want to make a life study of engineering is more than I can imagine.

"Yes, I know we let you take technology as your main subject, but we never thought you were so serious about it. When I was your age I had a passion for botany—but I never made it my main interest in life. Has Professor Chandras Ling been giving you ideas?"

Richard Peyton III blushed.

"Why shouldn't he? I know what my vocation is, and he agrees with me. You've read his report."

The artist waved several sheets of paper in the air, holding them between thumb and forefinger like some unpleasant insect.

"I have," he said grimly. " 'Shows very unusual mechanical ability—has done original work in subelectronic research,' et cetera, et cetera. Good heavens, I thought the human race had outgrown those toys centuries ago! Do you want to be a mechanic, first class, and go around attending to disabled robots? That's hardly a job for a boy of mine, not to mention the grandson of a World Councillor."

"I wish you wouldn't keep bringing Grandfather into this," said Richard Peyton III with mounting annoyance. "The fact that he was a statesman didn't prevent your becoming an artist. So why should you expect me to be either?"

The older man's spectacular golden beard began to bristle ominously.

"I don't care what you do as long as it's something we can be proud of. But why this craze for gadgets? We've got all the machines we need. The robot was perfected five hundred years ago; spaceships haven't changed for at least that time; I believe our present communications system is nearly eight hundred years old. So why change what's already perfect?"

"That's special pleading with a vengeance!" the young man replied. "Fancy an artist saying that anything's perfect! Father, I'm ashamed of you!"

"Don't split hairs. You know perfectly well what I mean. Our ancestors designed machines that provide us with everything we need. No doubt some of them might be a few per cent more efficient. But why worry? Can you mention a single important invention that the world lacks today?"

Richard Peyton III sighed.

"Listen, Father," he said patiently. "I've been studying history as well as engineering. About twelve centuries ago there were people who said that everything had been invented—and *that* was before the coming of electricity, let alone flying and astronautics. They just didn't look far enough ahead—their minds were rooted in the present.

"The same thing's happening today. For five hundred years the world's been living on the brains of the past. I'm prepared to admit that some lines of development have come to an end, but there are dozens of others that haven't even begun.

"Technically the world has stagnated. It's not a dark age, because we haven't forgotten anything. But we're marking time. Look at space travel. Nine hundred years ago we reached Pluto, and where are we now? Still at Pluto! When are we going to cross interstellar space?"

"Who wants to go to the stars, anyway?"

The boy made an exclamation of annoyance and jumped off the diamond block in his excitement.

"What a question to ask in this age! A thousand years ago people were saying, 'Who wants to go to the Moon?' Yes, I know it's unbelievable, but it's all there in the old books. Nowadays the Moon's only forty-five minutes away, and people like Harn Jansen work on Earth and live in Plato City.

"We take interplanetary travel for granted. One day we're going to do the same with *real* space travel. I could mention scores of other subjects that have come to a full stop simply because people think as you do and are content with what they've got."

"And why not?"

Peyton waved his arm around in the studio.

"Be serious, Father. Have you ever been satisfied with anything you've made? Only animals are contented."

The artist laughed ruefully.

"Maybe you're right. But that doesn't affect my argument. I still think you'll be wasting your life, and so does Grandfather." He looked a little embarrassed. "In fact, he's coming down to Earth especially to see you."

Peyton looked alarmed.

"Listen, Father, I've already told you what I think. I don't want to have to go through it all again. Because neither Grandfather nor the whole of the World Council will make me alter my mind."

It was a bombastic statement, and Peyton wondered if he really meant it. His father was just about to reply when a low musical note vibrated through the studio. A second later a mechanical voice spoke from the air.

"Your father to see you, Mr. Peyton."

He glanced at his son triumphantly.

"I should have added," he said, "that Grandfather was coming now. But I know your habit of disappearing when you're wanted."

The boy did not answer. He watched his father walk toward the door. Then his lips curved in a smile.

The single pane of glassite that fronted the studio was open, and he stepped out on to the balcony. Two miles below, the great concrete apron of the parking ground gleamed whitely in the sun, except where it was dotted with the teardrop shadows of grounded ships.

Peyton glanced back into the room. It was still empty, though he could hear his father's voice drifting through the door. He waited no longer. Placing his hand on the balustrade, he vaulted over into space.

Thirty seconds later two figures entered the studio and gazed around in surprise. *The* Richard Peyton, with no qualifying number, was a man who might have been taken for sixty, though that was less than a third of his actual age.

He was dressed in the purple robe worn by only twenty men on Earth and by fewer than a hundred in the entire Solar System. Authority seemed to radiate from him; by comparison, even his famous and self-assured son seemed fussy and inconsequential.

"Well, where is he?"

"Confound him! He's gone out the window. At least we can still say what we think of him."

Viciously, Richard Peyton II jerked up his wrist and dialed an eight-figure number on his personal communicator. The reply came almost instantly. In clear, impersonal tones an automatic voice repeated endlessly:

"My master is asleep. Please do not disturb. My master is asleep. Please do not disturb. . . ."

With an exclamation of annoyance Richard Peyton II switched off the instrument and turned to his father. The old man chuckled.

"Well, he thinks fast. He's beaten us there. We can't get hold of him until he chooses to press the clearing button. I certainly don't intend to chase him at my age."

There was silence for a moment as the two men gazed at each other with mixed expressions. Then, almost simultaneously, they began to laugh.

Peyton fell like a stone for a mile and a quarter before he switched on the neutralizer. The rush of air past him, though it made breathing difficult, was exhilarating. He was falling at less than a hundred and fifty miles an hour, but the impression of speed was enhanced by the smooth upward rush of the great building only a few yards away.

The gentle tug of the decelerator field slowed him some three hundred yards from the ground. He fell gently toward the lines of parked flyers ranged at the foot of the tower.

His own speedster was a small single-seat fully automatic machine. At least, it had been fully automatic when it was built three centuries ago, but its current owner had made so many illegal modifications to it that no one else in the world could have flown it and lived to tell the tale.

Peyton switched off the neutralizer belt—an amusing device which, although technically obsolete, still had interesting possibilities—and stepped into the airlock of his machine. Two minutes later the towers of the city were sinking below the rim of the world and the uninhabited Wild Lands were speeding beneath at four thousand miles an hour.

Peyton set his course westward and almost immediately was over the ocean. He could do nothing but wait; the ship would reach its goal automatically. He leaned back in the pilot's seat, thinking bitter thoughts and feeling sorry for himself.

He was more disturbed than he cared to admit. The fact that his family failed to share his technical interests had ceased to worry Peyton years ago. But this steadily growing opposition, which had now come to a head, was something quite new. He was completely unable to understand it.

Ten minutes later a single white pylon began to climb out of the ocean like the sword Excalibur rising from the lake. The city known to the world as Scientia, and to its more cynical inhabitants as Bat's Belfry, had been built eight centuries ago on an island far from the major land masses. The gesture had been one of independence, for the last traces of nationalism had still lingered in that far-off age.

Peyton grounded his ship on the landing apron and walked to the nearest entrance. The boom of the great waves, breaking on the rocks a hundred yards away, was a sound that never failed to impress him.

He paused for a moment at the opening, inhaling the salt air and watching the gulls and migrant birds circling the tower. They had used this speck of land as a resting place when man was still watching the dawn with puzzled eyes and wondering if it was a god.

The Bureau of Genetics occupied a hundred floors near the center of the tower. It had taken Peyton ten minutes to reach the City of Science. It required almost as long again to locate the man he wanted in the cubic miles of offices and laboratories.

Alan Henson II was still one of Peyton's closest friends, although he had left the University of Antarctica two years earlier and had been studying biogenetics rather than engineering. When Peyton was in trouble, which was not infrequently, he found his friend's calm common sense very reassuring. It was natural for him to fly to Scientia now, especially since Henson had sent him an urgent call only the day before.

The biologist was pleased and relieved to see Peyton, yet his welcome had an undercurrent of nervousness.

"I'm glad you've come; I've got some news that will interest you. But you look glum—what's the matter?"

Peyton told him, not without exaggeration. Henson was silent for a moment.

"So they've started already!" he said. "We might have expected it!"

"What do you mean?" asked Peyton in surprise.

The biologist opened a drawer and pulled out a sealed envelope. From it he extracted two plastic sheets in which were cut several hundred parallel slots of varying lengths. He handed one to his friend.

"Do you know what this is?"

"It looks like a character analysis."

"Correct. It happens to be yours."

"Oh! This is rather illegal, isn't it?"

"Never mind that. The key is printed along the bottom: it runs from Aesthetic Appreciation to Wit. The last column gives your Intelligence Quotient. Don't let it go to your head."

Peyton studied the card intently. Once, he flushed slightly.

"I don't see how you knew."

"Never mind," grinned Henson. "Now look at this analysis." He handed over a second card.

"Why, it's the same one!"

"Not quite, but very nearly."

"Whom does it belong to?"

Henson leaned back in his chair and measured out his words slowly.

"That analysis, Dick, belongs to your great-grandfather twenty-two times removed on the direct male line—the great Rolf Thordarsen."

Peyton took off like a rocket.

"What!"

"Don't shout the place down. We're discussing old times at college if anyone comes in."

"But—Thordarsen!"

"Well, if we go back far enough we've all got equally distinguished ancestors. But now you know why your grandfather is afraid of you."

"He's left it till rather late. I've practically finished my training."

"You can thank us for that. Normally our analysis goes back ten generations, twenty in special cases. It's a tremendous job. There are hundreds of millions of cards in the Inheritance Library, one for every man and woman who has lived since the twenty-third century. This coincidence was discovered quite accidentally about a month ago."

"*That's* when the trouble started. But I still don't understand what it's all about."

"Exactly what do you know, Dick, about your famous ancestor?"

"No more than anyone else, I suppose. I certainly don't know how or why he disappeared, if that's what you mean. Didn't he leave Earth?"

"No. He left the world, if you like, but he never left Earth. Very few people know this, Dick, but Rolf Thordarsen was the man who built Comarre."

Comarre! Peyton breathed the word through half-open lips, savoring its meaning and its strangeness. So it *did* exist, after all! Even that had been denied by some.

Henson was speaking again.

"I don't suppose you know very much about the Decadents. The history books have been rather carefully edited. But the whole story is linked up with the end of the Second Electronic Age. . . ."

▼

Twenty thousand miles above the surface of the Earth, the artificial moon that housed the World Council was spinning on its eternal orbit. The roof of the Council Chamber was one flawless sheet of crystallite; when the

members of the Council were in session it seemed as if
there was nothing between them and the great globe
spinning far below.

The symbolism was profound. No narrow parochial
viewpoint could long survive in such a setting. Here, if
anywhere, the minds of men would surely produce their
greatest works.

Richard Peyton the Elder had spent his life guiding
the destinies of Earth. For five hundred years the human
race had known peace and had lacked nothing that art or
science could provide. The men who ruled the planet
could be proud of their work.

Yet the old statesman was uneasy. Perhaps the changes
that lay ahead were already casting their shadows before
them. Perhaps he felt, if only with his subconscious mind,
that the five centuries of tranquillity were drawing to a
close.

He switched on his writing machine and began to dic-
tate.

The First Electronic Age, Peyton knew, had begun in
1908, more than eleven centuries before, with De
Forest's invention of the triode. The same fabulous century that had seen the coming of the World State, the
airplane, the spaceship, and atomic power had witnessed
the invention of all the fundamental thermionic devices
that made possible the civilization he knew.

The Second Electronic Age had come five hundred
years later. It had been started not by the physicists but
by the doctors and psychologists. For nearly five centuries
they had been recording the electric currents that flow in
the brain during the processes of thought. The analysis
had been appallingly complex, but it had been completed
after generations of toil. When it was finished the way lay
open for the first machines that could read the human
mind.

But this was only the beginning. Once man had discovered the mechanism of his own brain he could go further. He could reproduce it, using transistors and circuit networks instead of living cells.

Toward the end of the twenty-fifth century, the first thinking machines were built. They were very crude, a hundred square yards of equipment being required to do the work of a cubic centimeter of human brain. But once the first step had been taken it was not long before the mechanical brain was perfected and brought into general use.

It could perform only the lower grades of intellectual work and it lacked such purely human characteristics as initiative, intuition, and all emotions. However, in circumstances which seldom varied, where its limitations were not serious, it could do all that a man could do.

The coming of the metal brains had brought one of the great crises in human civilization. Though men had still to carry out all the higher duties of statesmanship and the control of society, all the immense mass of routine administration had been taken over by the robots. Man had achieved freedom at last. No longer did he have to rack his brains planning complex transport schedules, deciding production programs, and balancing budgets. The machines, which had taken over all manual labor centuries before, had made their second great contribution to society.

The effect on human affairs was immense, and men reacted to the new situation in two ways. There were those who used their new-found freedom nobly in the pursuits which had always attracted the highest minds: the quest for beauty and truth, still as elusive as when the Acropolis was built.

But there were others who thought differently. At last, they said, the curse of Adam is lifted forever. Now we can build cities where the machines will care for our every need as soon as the thought enters our minds—sooner, since the analyzers can read even the buried desires of the subconscious. The aim of all life is pleasure and the pursuit of happiness. Man has earned the right to that. We are tired of this unending struggle for knowledge and the blind desire to bridge space to the stars.

It was the ancient dream of the Lotus Eaters, a dream as old as Man. Now, for the first time, it could be realized. For a while there were not many who shared it. The fires of the Second Renaissance had not yet begun to flicker and die. But as the years passed, the Decadents drew more and more to their way of thinking. In hidden places on the inner planets they built the cities of their dreams.

For a century they flourished like strange exotic flowers, until the almost religious fervor that inspired their building had died. They lingered for a generation more. Then, one by one, they faded from human knowledge. Dying, they left behind a host of fables and legends which had grown with the passing centuries.

Only one such city had been built on Earth, and there were mysteries about it that the outer world had never solved. For purposes of its own, the World Council had destroyed all knowledge of the place. Its location was a mystery. Some said it was in the Arctic wastes; others believed it to be hidden on the bed of the Pacific. Nothing was certain but its name—Comarre.

▼

Henson paused in his recital.

"So far I have told you nothing new, nothing that isn't common knowledge. The rest of the story is a secret to the World Council and perhaps a hundred men of Scientia.

"Rolf Thordarsen, as you know, was the greatest mechanical genius the world has ever known. Not even Edison can be compared with him. He laid the foundations of robot engineering and built the first of the practical thought-machines.

"His laboratories poured out a stream of brilliant inventions for over twenty years. Then, suddenly, he disappeared. The story was put out that he tried to reach the stars. This is what really happened:

"Thordarsen believed that his robots—the machines that still run our civilization—were only a beginning. He went to the World Council with certain proposals which would have changed the face of human society. What those changes are we do not know, but Thordarsen believed that unless they were adopted the race would eventually come to a dead end—as, indeed, many of us think it has.

"The Council disagreed violently. At that time, you see, the robot was just being integrated into civilization and stability was slowly returning—the stability that has been maintained for five hundred years.

"Thordarsen was bitterly disappointed. With the flair they had for attracting genius the Decadents got hold of him and persuaded him to renounce the world. He was the only man who could convert their dreams into reality."

"And did he?"

"No one knows. But Comarre was built—that is certain. We know where it is—and so does the World Council. There are some things that cannot be kept secret."

That was true, thought Peyton. Even in this age people still disappeared and it was rumored that they had gone in search of the dream city. Indeed, the phrase "He's gone to Comarre" had become such a part of the language that its meaning was almost forgotten.

Henson leaned forward and spoke with mounting earnestness.

"This is the strange part. The World Council could destroy Comarre, but it won't do so. The belief that Comarre exists has a definite stabilizing influence on society. In spite of all our efforts, we still have psychopaths. It's no difficult matter to give them hints, under hypnosis, about Comarre. They may never find it but the quest will keep them harmless.

"In the early days, soon after the city was founded, the Council sent its agents into Comarre. None of them ever returned. There was no foul play; they just preferred to remain. That's known definitely because they sent messages back. I suppose the Decadents realized that the Council would tear the place down if its agents were detained deliberately.

"I've seen some of those messages. They are extraordinary. There's only one word for them: exalted. Dick, there was something in Comarre that could make a man forget the outer world, his friends, his family—everything! Try to imagine what that means!

"Later, when it was certain that none of the Decadents could still be alive, the Council tried again. It was still trying up to fifty years ago. But to this day no one has ever returned from Comarre."

As Richard Peyton spoke, the waiting robot analyzed his words into their phonetic groups, inserted the punctuation, and automatically routed the minute to the correct electronic files.

"Copy to President and my personal file.

"Your Minute of the 22nd and our conversation this morning.

"I have seen my son, but R. P. III evaded me. He is completely determined, and we will only do harm by trying to coerce him. Thordarsen should have taught us that lesson.

"My suggestion is that we earn his gratitude by giving him all the assistance he needs. Then we can direct him along safe lines of research. As long as he never discovers that R. T. was his ancestor, there should be no danger. In spite of character similarities, it is unlikely that he will try to repeat R. T.'s work.

"Above all, we must ensure that he never locates or visits Comarre. If that happens, no one can foresee the consequences."

Henson stopped his narrative, but his friend said nothing. He was too spellbound to interrupt, and, after a minute, the other continued.

"That brings us up to the present and to you. The World Council, Dick, discovered your inheritance a month ago. We're sorry we told them, but it's too late now. Genetically, you're a reincarnation of Thordarsen in the only scientific sense of the word. One of Nature's longest odds has come off, as it does every few hundred years in some family or another.

"You, Dick, could carry on the work Thordarsen was compelled to drop—whatever that work was. Perhaps it's lost forever, but if any trace of it exists, the secret lies in Comarre. The World Council knows that. That is why it is trying to deflect you from your destiny.

"Don't be bitter about it. On the Council are some of the noblest minds the human race has yet produced. They mean you no harm, and none will ever befall you. But they are passionately anxious to preserve the present structure of society, which they believe to be the best."

Slowly, Peyton rose to his feet. For a moment, it seemed as if he were a neutral, exterior observer, watching this lay figure called Richard Peyton III, now no longer a man, but a symbol, one of the keys to the future of the world. It took a positive mental effort to reidentify himself.

His friend was watching him silently.

"There's something else you haven't told me, Alan. How do you know all this?"

Henson smiled.

"I was waiting for that. I'm only the mouthpiece, chosen because I know you. Who the others are I can't say, even to you. But they include quite a number of the scientists I know you admire.

"There has always been a friendly rivalry between the Council and the scientists who serve it, but in the last few years our viewpoints have drifted farther apart. Many of us believe that the present age, which the Council thinks will last forever, is only an interregnum. We believe that too long a period of stability will cause decadence. The Council's psychologists are confident they can prevent it."

Peyton's eyes gleamed.

"That's what I've been saying! Can I join you?"

"Later. There's work to be done first. You see, we are revolutionaries of a sort. We are going to start one or two social reactions, and when we've finished the danger of racial decadence will be postponed for thousands of years. You, Dick, are one of our catalysts. Not the only one, I might say."

He paused for a moment.

"Even if Comarre comes to nothing, we have another card up our sleeve. In fifty years, we hope to have perfected the interstellar drive."

"At last!" said Peyton. "What will you do then?"

"We'll present it to the Council and say, 'Here you are—now you can go to the stars. Aren't we good boys?' And the Council will just have to give a sickly smile and start uprooting civilization. Once we've achieved interstellar travel, we shall have an expanding society again and stagnation will be indefinitely postponed."

"I hope I live to see it," said Peyton. "But what do you want me to do now?"

"Just this: we want you to go into Comarre to find

what's there. Where others have failed, we believe you can succeed. All the plans have been made."

"And where is Comarre?"

Henson smiled.

"It's simple, really. There was only one place it could be—the only place over which no aircraft can fly, where no one lives, where all travel is on foot. It's in the Great Reservation."

The old man switched off the writing machine. Overhead—or below; it was all the same—the great crescent of Earth was blotting out the stars. In its eternal circling the little moon had overtaken the terminator and was plunging into night. Here and there the darkling land below was dotted with the lights of cities.

The sight filled the old man with sadness. It reminded him that his own life was coming to a close—and it seemed to foretell the end of the culture he had sought to protect. Perhaps, after all, the young scientists were right. The long rest was ending and the world was moving to new goals that he would never see.

It was night when Peyton's ship came westward over the Indian Ocean. The eye could see nothing far below but the white line of breakers against the African coast, but the navigation screen showed every detail of the land beneath. Night, of course, was no protection or safeguard now, but it meant that no human eye would see him. As for the machines that should be watching—well, others had taken care of them. There were many, it seemed, who thought as Henson did.

The plan had been skillfully conceived. The details had been worked out with loving care by people who had obviously enjoyed themselves. He was to land the ship at the edge of the forest, as near to the power barrier as he could.

Not even his unknown friends could switch off the barrier without arousing suspicion. Luckily it was only about twenty miles to Comarre from the edge of the screen, over fairly open country. He would have to finish the journey afoot.

There was a great crackling of branches as the little ship settled down into the unseen forest. It came to rest on an even keel, and Peyton switched off the dim cabin lights and peered out of the window. He could see nothing. Remembering what he had been told, he did not open the door. He made himself as comfortable as he could and settled down to await the dawn.

He awoke with brilliant sunlight shining full in his eyes. Quickly climbing into the equipment his friends had provided, he opened the cabin door and stepped into the forest.

The landing place had been carefully chosen, and it was not difficult to scramble through to the open country a few yards away. Ahead lay small grass-covered hills dotted with occasional clusters of slender trees. The day was mild, though it was summer and the equator was not far away. Eight hundred years of climatic control and the great artificial lakes that had drowned the deserts had seen to that.

For almost the first time in his life Peyton was experiencing Nature as it had been in the days before Man existed. Yet it was not the wildness of the scene that he found so strange. Peyton had never known silence. Always there had been the murmur of machines or the faraway whisper of speeding liners, heard faintly from the towering heights of the stratosphere.

Here there were none of these sounds, for no machines could cross the power barrier that surrounded the Reservation. There was only the wind in the grass and the half-audible medley of insect voices. Peyton found the silence unnerving and did what almost any man of his time would have done. He pressed the button of his personal radio that selected the background-music band.

So, mile after mile, Peyton walked steadily through the undulating country of the Great Reservation, the largest area of natural territory remaining on the surface of the globe. Walking was easy, for the neutralizers built into his equipment almost nullified its weight. He carried with him that mist of unobtrusive music that had been the background of men's lives almost since the discovery of radio. Although he had only to flick a dial to get in touch with anyone on the planet, he quite sincerely imagined himself to be alone in the heart of Nature, and for a moment he felt all the emotions that Stanley or Livingstone must have experienced when they first entered this same land more than a thousand years ago.

Luckily Peyton was a good walker, and by noon had

covered half the distance to his goal. He rested for his midday meal under a cluster of imported Martian conifers, which would have brought baffled consternation to an old-time explorer. In his ignorance Peyton took them completely for granted.

He had accumulated a small pile of empty cans when he noticed an object moving swiftly over the plain in the direction from which he had come. It was too far away to be recognized. Not until it was obviously approaching him did he bother to get up to get a clearer view of it. So far he had seen no animals—though plenty of animals had seen him—and he watched the newcomer with interest.

Peyton had never seen a lion before, but he had no difficulty in recognizing the magnificent beast that was bounding toward him. It was to his credit that he glanced only once at the tree overhead. Then he stood his ground firmly.

There were, he knew, no really dangerous animals in the world any more. The Reservation was something between a vast biological laboratory and a national park, visited by thousands of people every year. It was generally understood that if one left the inhabitants alone, they would reciprocate. On the whole, the arrangement worked smoothly.

The animal was certainly anxious to be friendly. It trotted straight toward him and began to rub itself affectionately against his side. When Peyton got up again, it was taking a great deal of interest in his empty food cans. Presently it turned toward him with an expression that was irresistible.

Peyton laughed, opened a fresh can, and laid the contents carefully on a flat stone. The lion accepted the tribute with relish, and while it was eating Peyton ruffled through the index of the official guide which his unknown supporters had thoughtfully provided.

There were several pages about lions, with photographs

for the benefit of extraterrestrial visitors. The information was reassuring. A thousand years of scientific breeding had greatly improved the King of Beasts. He had eaten only a dozen people in the last century: in ten of the cases the subsequent enquiry had exonerated him from blame and the other two were "not proved."

But the book said nothing about unwanted lions and the best ways of disposing of them. Nor did it hint that they were normally as friendly as this specimen.

Peyton was not particularly observant. It was some time before he noticed the thin metal band around the lion's right forepaw. It bore a series of numbers and letters, followed by the official stamp of the Reservation.

This was no wild animal; perhaps all its youth had been spent among men. It was probably one of the famous superlions the biologists had been breeding and then releasing to improve the race. Some of them were almost as intelligent as dogs, according to the reports that Peyton had seen.

He quickly discovered that it could understand many simple words, particularly those relating to food. Even for this era it was a splendid beast, a good foot taller than its scrawny ancestors of ten centuries before.

When Peyton started on his journey again, the lion trotted by his side. He doubted if its friendship was worth more than a pound of synthetic beef, but it was pleasant to have someone to talk to—someone, moreover, who made no attempt to contradict him. After profound and concentrated thought, he decided that "Leo" would be a suitable name for his new acquaintance.

Peyton had walked a few hundred yards when suddenly there was a blinding flash in the air before him. Though he realized immediately what it was, he was startled, and stopped, blinking. Leo had fled precipitately and was already out of sight. He would not, Peyton thought, be of much use in an emergency. Later he was to revise this judgment.

When his eyes had reocvered, Peyton found himself looking at a multicolored notice, burning in letters of fire. It hung steadily in the air and read:

WARNING!
YOU ARE NOW APPROACHING
RESTRICTED TERRITORY!
TURN BACK!

By Order,
World Council in Session

Peyton regarded the notice thoughtfully for a few moments. Then he looked around for the projector. It was in a metal box, not very effectively hidden at the side of the road. He quickly unlocked it with the universal keys a trusting Electronics Commission had given him on his first graduation.

After a few minutes' inspection he breathed a sigh of relief. The projector was a simple capacity-operated device. Anything coming along the road would actuate it. There was a photographic recorder, but it had been disconnected. Peyton was not surprised, for every passing animal would have operated the device. This was fortunate. It meant that no one need ever know that Richard Peyton III had once walked along this road.

He shouted to Leo, who came slowly back, looking rather ashamed of himself. The sign had disappeared, and Peyton held the relays open to prevent its reappearance as Leo passed by. Then he relocked the door and continued on his way, wondering what would happen next.

A hundred yards farther on, a disembodied voice began to speak to him severely. It told him nothing new, but the voice threatened a number of minor penalties, some of which were not unfamiliar to him.

It was amusing to watch Leo's face as he tried to locate

the source of the sound. Once again Peyton searched for the projector and checked it before proceeding. It would be safer, he thought, to leave the road altogether. There might be recording devices farther along it.

With some difficulty he induced Leo to remain on the metal surface while he himself walked along the barren ground bordering the road. In the next quarter of a mile the lion set off two more electronic booby traps. The last one seemed to have given up persuasion. It said simply:

BEWARE OF WILD LIONS

Peyton looked at Leo and began to laugh. Leo couldn't see the joke but he joined in politely. Behind them the automatic sign faded out with a last despairing flicker.

Peyton wondered why the signs were there at all. Perhaps they were intended to scare away accidental visitors. Those who knew the goal would hardly be deflected by them.

The road made a sudden right-angle turn—and there before him was Comarre. It was strange that something he had been expecting could give him such a shock. Ahead lay an immense clearing in the jungle, half filled by a black metallic structure.

The city was shaped like a terraced cone, perhaps eight hundred yards high and a thousand across at the base. How much was underground, Peyton could not guess. He halted, overwhelmed by the size and strangeness of the enormous building. Then, slowly, he began to walk toward it.

Like a beast of prey crouching in its lair, the city lay waiting. Though its guests were now very few, it was ready to receive them, whoever they might be. Sometimes they turned back at the first warning, sometimes at the second. A few had reached the very entrance before their resolution failed them. But most, having come so far, had entered willingly enough.

So Peyton reached the marble steps that led up to the towering metal wall and the curious black hole that seemed to be the only entrance. Leo trotted quietly beside him, taking little notice of his strange surroundings.

Peyton stopped at the foot of the stairs and dialed a number in his communicator. He waited until the acknowledgment tone came and then spoke slowly into the microphone.

"The fly is entering the parlor."

He repeated it twice, feeling rather a fool. Someone, he thought, had a perverted sense of humor.

There was no reply. That had been part of the arrangement. But he had no doubt that the message had been received, probably in some laboratory in Scientia, since the number he had dialed had a Western Hemisphere coding.

Peyton opened his biggest can of meat and spread it out on the marble. He entwined his fingers in the lion's mane and twisted it playfully.

"I guess you'd better stay here, Leo," he said. "I may be gone quite some time. Don't try to follow me."

At the top of the steps, he looked back. Rather to his relief the lion had made no attempt to follow. It was sitting on its haunches, looking at him pathetically. Peyton waved and turned away.

There was no door, only a plain black hole in the curving metal surface. That was puzzling, and Peyton wondered how the builders had expected to keep animals from wandering in. Then something about the opening attracted his attention.

It was *too* black. Although the wall was in shadow, the entrance had no right to be as dark as this. He took a coin from his pocket and tossed it into the aperture. The sound of its fall reassured him, and he stepped forward.

The delicately adjusted discriminator circuits had ignored the coin, as they had ignored all the stray animals that had entered this dark portal. But the presence of a

*human mind had been enough to trip the relays. For a
fraction of a second the screen through which Peyton was
moving throbbed with power. Then it became inert again.*

It seemed to Peyton that his foot took a long time to
reach the ground, but that was the least of his worries.
Far more surprising was the instantaneous transition from
darkness to sudden light, from the somewhat oppressive
heat of the jungle to a temperature that seemed almost
chilly by comparison. The change was so abrupt that it
left him gasping. Filled with a feeling of distinct unease
he turned toward the archway through which he had just
come.

It was no longer there. It never had been there. He was
standing on a raised metal dais at the exact center of a
large circular room with a dozen pointed archways
around its circumference. He might have come through
any one of them—if only they had not all been forty yards
away.

For a moment Peyton was seized with panic. He felt his
heart pounding, and something odd was happening to his
legs. Feeling very much alone, he sat down on the dais
and began to consider the situation logically.

Something had transported him instantly from the black doorway to the center of the room. There could be only two explanations, both equally fantastic. Either something was very wrong with space inside Comarre, or else its builders had mastered the secret of matter transmission.

Ever since men had learned to send sound and sight by radio, they had dreamed of transmitting matter by the same means. Peyton looked at the dais on which he was standing. It might easily hold electronic equipment—and there was a very curious bulge in the ceiling above him.

However it was done, he could imagine no better way of ignoring unwanted visitors. Rather hurriedly, he scrambled off the dais. It was not the sort of place where he cared to linger.

It was disturbing to realize that he now had no means of leaving without the co-operation of the machine that had brought him here. He decided to worry about one thing at a time. When he had finished his exploration, he should have mastered this and all the other secrets of Comarre.

He was not really conceited. Between Peyton and the makers of the city lay five centuries of research. Although he might find much that was new to him, there would be nothing that he could not understand. Choosing one of the exits at random, he began his exploration of the city.

The machines were watching, biding their time. They had been built to serve one purpose, and that purpose they were still fulfilling blindly. Long ago they had brought the peace of oblivion to the weary minds of their builders. That oblivion they could still bring to all who entered the city of Comarre.

The instruments had begun their analysis when Peyton stepped in from the forest. It was not a task that could be done swiftly, this dissection of a human mind, with all its hopes, desires, and fears. The synthesizers would not come into operation for hours yet. Until then the guest would be entertained while the more lavish hospitality was being prepared.

The elusive visitor gave the little robot a lot of trouble before it finally located him, for Peyton was moving rapidly from room to room in his exploration of the city. Presently the machine came to a halt in the center of a small circular room lined with magnetic switches and lit by a single glow tube.

According to its instruments, Peyton was only a few feet away, but its four eye lenses could see no sign of him. Puzzled, it stood motionless, silent except for the faint whisper of its motors and the occasional snicker of a relay.

Standing on a catwalk ten feet from the ground, Peyton was watching the machine with great interest. He saw a shining metal cylinder rising from a thick base plate mounted on small driving wheels. There were no limbs of any kind: the cylinder was unbroken except for the circlet of eye lenses and a series of small metal sound grilles.

It was amusing to watch the machine's perplexity as its tiny mind wrestled with two conflicting sets of information. Although it knew that Peyton must be in the room, its eyes told it that the place was empty. It began to scamper around in small circles, until Peyton took pity on it and descended from the catwalk. Immediately the machine ceased its gyrations and began to deliver its address of welcome.

"I am A-Five. I will take you wherever you wish to go. Please give me your orders in standard robot vocab."

Peyton was rather disappointed. It was a perfectly standard robot, and he had hoped for something better in the city Thordarsen had built. But the machine could be very useful if he employed it properly.

"Thank you," he said, unnecessarily. "Please take me to the living quarters."

Although Peyton was now certain that the city was completely automatic, there was still the possibility that it held some human life. There might be others here who could help him in his quest, though the absence of opposition was perhaps as much as he could hope for.

Without a word the little machine spun around on its driving wheels and rolled out of the room. The corridor along which it led Peyton ended at a beautifully carved door, which he had already tried in vain to open. Apparently A-Five knew its secret—for at their approach the thick metal plate slid silently aside. The robot rolled forward into a small, boxlike chamber.

Peyton wondered if they had entered another of the matter transmitters, but quickly discovered that it was nothing more unusual than an elevator. Judging by the time of ascent, it must have taken them almost to the top of the city. When the doors slid open it seemed to Peyton that he was in another world.

The corridors in which he had first found himself were drab and undecorated, purely utilitarian. In contrast, these spacious halls and assembly rooms were furnished with the utmost luxury. The twenty-sixth century had been a period of florid decoration and coloring, much despised by subsequent ages. But the Decadents had gone far beyond their own period. They had taxed the resources of psychology as well as art when they designed Comarre.

One could have spent a lifetime without exhausting all

the murals, the carvings and paintings, the intricate tapestries which still seemed as brilliant as when they had been made. It seemed utterly wrong that so wonderful a place should be deserted and hidden from the world. Peyton almost forgot all his scientific zeal, and hurried like a child from marvel to marvel.

Here were works of genius, perhaps as great as any the world had ever known. But it was a sick and despairing genius, one that had lost faith in itself while still retaining an immense technical skill. For the first time Peyton truly understood why the builders of Comarre had been given their name.

The art of the Decadents at once repelled and fascinated him. It was not evil, for it was completely detached from moral standards. Perhaps its dominant characteristics were weariness and disillusion. After a while Peyton, who had never thought himself very sensitive to visual art, began to feel a subtle depression creeping into his soul. Yet he found it quite impossible to tear himself away.

At last Peyton turned to the robot again.

"Does anyone live here now?"

"Yes."

"Where are they?"

"Sleeping."

Somehow that seemed a perfectly natural reply. Peyton felt very tired. For the last hour it had been a struggle to remain awake. Something seemed to be compelling sleep, almost willing it upon him. Tomorrow would be time enough to learn the secrets he had come to find. For the moment he wanted nothing but sleep.

He followed automatically when the robot led him out of the spacious halls into a long corridor lined with metal doors, each bearing a half-familiar symbol Peyton could not quite recognize. His sleepy mind was still wrestling halfheartedly with the problem when the machine halted before one of the doors, which slid silently open.

The heavily draped couch in the darkened room was irresistible. Peyton stumbled toward it automatically. As he sank down into sleep, a glow of satisfaction warned his mind. He had recognized the symbol on the door, though his brain was too tired to understand its significance.

It was the poppy.

There was no guile, no malevolence in the working of the city. Impersonally it was fulfilling the tasks to which it had been dedicated. All who had entered Comarre had willingly embraced its gifts. This visitor was the first who had ever ignored them.

The integrators had been ready for hours, but the restless, probing mind had eluded them. They could afford to wait, as they had done these last five hundred years.

And now the defenses of this strangely stubborn mind were crumbling as Richard Peyton sank peacefully to sleep. Far down in the heart of Comarre a relay tripped, and complex, slowly fluctuating currents began to ebb and flow through banks of vacuum tubes. The consciousness that had been Richard Peyton III ceased to exist.

Peyton had fallen asleep instantly. For a while complete oblivion claimed him. Then faint wisps of consciousness began to return. And then, as always, he began to dream.

It was strange that his favorite dream should have come into his mind, and it was more vivid now than it had ever been before. All his life Peyton had loved the sea, and once he had seen the unbelievable beauty of the Pacific islands from the observation deck of a low-flying liner. He had never visited them, but he had often wished that he could spend his life on some remote and peaceful isle with no care for the future or the world.

It was a dream that almost all men had known at some

time in their lives, but Peyton was sufficiently sensible to realize that two months of such an existence would have driven him back to civilization, half crazy with boredom. However, his dreams were never worried by such considerations, and once more he was lying beneath waving palms, the surf drumming on the reef beyond a lagoon that framed the sun in an azure mirror.

The dream was extraordinarily vivid, so much so that even in his sleep Peyton found himself thinking that no dream had any right to be so real. Then it ceased, so abruptly that there seemed to be a definite rift in his thoughts. The interruption jolted him back to consciousness.

Bitterly disappointed, Peyton lay for a while with his eyes tightly closed, trying to recapture the lost paradise. But it was useless. Something was beating against his brain, keeping him from sleep. Moreover, his couch had suddenly become very hard and uncomfortable. Reluctantly he turned his mind toward the interruption.

Peyton had always been a realist and had never been troubled by philosophical doubts, so the shock was far greater than it might have been to many less intelligent minds. Never before had he found himself doubting his own sanity, but he did so now. For the sound that had awakened him was the drumming of the waves against the reef. He was lying on the golden sand beside the lagoon. Around him, the wind was sighing through the palms, its warm fingers caressing him gently.

For a moment, Peyton could only imagine that he was still dreaming. But this time there could be no real doubt. While one is sane, reality can never be mistaken for a dream. This was real if anything in the universe was real.

Slowly the sense of wonder began to fade. He rose to his feet, the sand showering from him in a golden rain.

Shielding his eyes against the sun, he stared along the beach.

He did not stop to wonder why the place should be so familiar. It seemed natural enough to know that the village was a little farther along the bay. Presently he would rejoin his friends, from whom he had been separated for a little while in a world he was swiftly forgetting.

There was a fading memory of a young engineer—even the name escaped him now—who had once aspired to fame and wisdom. In that other life, he had known this foolish person well, but now he could never explain to him the vanity of his ambitions.

He began to wander idly along the beach, the last vague recollections of his shadow life sloughing from him with every footstep, as the details of a dream fade into the light of day.

On the other side of the world three very worried scientists were waiting in a deserted laboratory, their eyes on a multichannel communicator of unusual design. The machine had been silent for nine hours. No one had expected a message in the first eight, but the prearranged signal was now more than an hour overdue.

Alan Henson jumped to his feet with a gesture of impatience.

"We've got to do something! I'm going to call him."

The other two scientists looked at each other nervously.

"The call may be traced!"

"Not unless they're actually watching us. Even if they are, I'll say nothing unusual. Peyton will understand, if he can answer at all. . . ."

If Richard Peyton had ever known time, that knowledge was forgotten now. Only the present was real, for both past and future lay hidden behind an impenetrable screen, as a great landscape may be concealed by a driving wall of rain.

In his enjoyment of the present Peyton was utterly content. Nothing at all was left of the restless driving spirit that had once set out, a little uncertainly, to conquer fresh fields of knowledge. He had no use for knowledge now.

Later he was never able to recollect anything of his life on the island. He had known many companions, but their names and faces had vanished beyond recall. Love, peace of mind, happiness—all were his for a brief moment of time. And yet he could remember no more than the last few moments of his life in paradise.

Strange that it should have ended as it began. Once more he was by the side of the lagoon, but this time it was night and he was not alone. The moon that seemed always to be full rode low above the ocean, and its long silver band stretched far away to the edge of the world. The stars that never changed their places glowed unblinking in the sky like brilliant jewels, more glorious than the forgotten stars of Earth.

But Peyton's thoughts were intent on other beauty, and once again he bent toward the figure lying on the sand that was no more golden than the hair strewn carelessly across it.

Then paradise trembled and dissolved around him. He gave a great cry of anguish as everything he loved was wrenched away. Only the swiftness of the transition saved his mind. When it was over, he felt as Adam must have when the gates of Eden clanged forever shut behind him.

But the sound that had brought him back was the most commonplace in all the world. Perhaps, indeed, no other could have reached his mind in its place of hiding. It was only the shrilling of his communicator set as it lay on the floor beside his couch, here in the darkened room in the city of Comarre.

The clangor died away as he reached out automatically to press the receiving switch. He must have made some answer that satisfied his unknown caller—who was Alan Henson?—for after a very short time the circuit was cleared. Still dazed, Peyton sat on the couch, holding his head in his hands and trying to reorient his life.

He had not been dreaming; he was sure of that. Rather, it was as if he had been living a second life and now he was returning to his old existence as might a man recovering from amnesia. Though he was still dazed, one clear conviction came into his mind. He must never again sleep in Comarre.

Slowly the will and character of Richard Peyton III returned from their banishment. Unsteadily he rose to his feet and made his way out of the room. Once again he found himself in the long corridor with its hundreds of identical doors. With new understanding he looked at the symbol carved upon them.

He scarcely noticed where he was going. His mind was fixed too intently on the problem before him. As he walked, his brain cleared, and slowly understanding came. For the moment it was only a theory, but soon he would put it to the test.

The human mind was a delicate, sheltered thing, having no direct contact with the world and gathering all its knowledge and experience through the body's senses. It was possible to record and store thoughts and emotions as earlier men had once recorded sound on miles of wire.

If those thoughts were projected into another mind, when the body was unconscious and all its senses numbed, that brain would think it was experiencing reality. There was no way in which it could detect the deception, any more than one can distinguish a perfectly recorded symphony from the original performance.

All this had been known for centuries, but the builders of Comarre had used the knowledge as no one in the world had ever done before. Somewhere in the city there must be machines that could analyze every thought and desire of those who entered. Elsewhere the city's makers must have stored every sensation and experience a human mind could know. From this raw material all possible futures could be constructed.

Now at last Peyton understood the measure of the genius that had gone into the making of Comarre. The machines had analyzed his deepest thoughts and built for him a world based on his subconscious desires. Then, when the chance had come, they had taken control of his mind and injected into it all he had experienced.

No wonder that everything he had ever longed for had been his in that already half-forgotten paradise. And no wonder that through the ages so many had sought the peace only Comarre could bring!

Peyton had become himself again by the time the sound of wheels made him look over his shoulder. The little robot that had been his guide was returning. No doubt the great machines that controlled it were wondering what had happened to its charge. Peyton waited, a thought slowly forming in his mind.

A-Five started all over again with its set speech. It seemed very incongruous now to find so simple a machine in this place where automatronics had reached their ultimate development. Then Peyton realized that perhaps the robot was deliberately uncomplicated. There was little purpose in using a complex machine where a simple one would serve as well—or better.

Peyton ignored the now familiar speech. All robots, he knew, must obey human commands unless other humans had previously given them orders to the contrary. Even the projectors of the city, he thought wryly, had obeyed the unknown and unspoken commands of his own subconscious mind.

"Lead me to the thought projectors," he commanded.

As he had expected, the robot did not move. It merely replied, "I do not understand."

Peyton's spirits began to revive as he felt himself once more master of the situation.

"Come here and do not move again until I give the order."

The robot's selectors and relays considered the instructions. They could find no countermanding order. Slowly the little machine rolled forward on its wheels. It had committed itself—there was no turning back now. It could not move again until Peyton ordered it to do so or something overrode his commands. Robot hypnosis was a very old trick, much beloved by mischievous small boys.

Swiftly, Peyton emptied his bag of the tools no engineer was ever without: the universal screw driver, the expanding wrench, the automatic drill, and, most important of all, the atomic cutter that could eat through the thickest metal in a matter of seconds. Then, with a skill born of long practice, he went to work on the unsuspecting machine.

Luckily the robot had been built for easy servicing, and could be opened with little difficulty. There was nothing unfamiliar about the controls, and it did not take Peyton long to find the locomotor mechanism. Now, whatever happened, the machine could not escape. It was crippled.

Next he blinded it and, one by one, tracked down its other electrical senses and put them out of commission. Soon the little machine was no more than a cylinder full of complicated junk. Feeling like a small boy who has just made a wanton attack on a defenseless grandfather clock, Peyton sat down and waited for what he knew must happen.

It was a little inconsiderate of him to sabotage the robot so far from the main machine levels. The robot-transporter took nearly fifteen minutes to work its way up from the depths. Peyton heard the rumble of its wheels in the distance and knew that his calculations had been correct. The breakdown party was on the way.

The transporter was a simple carrying machine, with a set of arms that could grasp and hold a damaged robot. It seemed to be blind, though no doubt its special senses were quite sufficient for its purpose.

Peyton waited until it had collected the unfortunate A-Five. Then he jumped aboard, keeping well away from the mechanical limbs. He had no desire to be mistaken for another distressed robot. Fortunately the big machine took no notice of him at all.

So Peyton descended through level after level of the great building, past the living quarters, through the room in which he had first found himself, and lower yet into regions he had never before seen. As he descended, the character of the city changed around him.

Gone now were the luxury and opulence of the higher levels, replaced by a no man's land of bleak passageways that were little more than giant cable ducts. Presently these, too, came to an end. The conveyor passed through a set of great sliding doors—and he had reached his goal.

The rows of relay panels and selector mechanisms seemed endless, but though Peyton was tempted to jump off his unwitting steed, he waited until the main control panels came into sight. Then he climbed off the conveyor and watched it disappear into the distance toward some still more remote part of the city.

He wondered how long it would take the superautomata to repair A-Five. His sabotage had been very thorough, and he rather thought the little machine was heading for the scrap heap. Then, feeling like a starving man suddenly confronted by a banquet, he began his examination of the city's wonders.

In the next five hours he paused only once to send the routine signal back to his friends. He wished he could tell of his success, but the risk was too great. After prodigies of circuit tracing he had discovered the functions of the main units and was beginning to investigate some of the secondary equipment.

It was just as he had expected. The thought analyzers and projectors lay on the floor immediately above, and could be controlled from, his central installation. How they worked he had no conception: it might well take months to uncover all their secrets. But he had identified them and thought he could probably switch them off if necessary.

A little later he discovered the thought monitor. It was a small machine, rather like an ancient manual telephone switchboard, but very much more complex. The operator's seat was a curious structure, insulated from the ground and roofed by a network of wires and crystal bars. It was the first machine he had discovered that was obviously intended for direct human use. Probably the first engineers had built it to set up the equipment in the early days of the city.

Peyton would not have risked using the thought monitor if detailed instructions had not been printed on its control panel. After some experimenting he plugged in to one of the circuits and slowly increased the power, keeping the intensity control well below the red danger mark.

It was as well that he did so, for the sensation was a shattering one. He still retained his own personality, but superimposed on his own thoughts were ideas and images that were utterly foreign to him. He was looking at another world, through the windows of an alien mind.

It was as though his body were in two places at once, though the sensations of his second personality were much less vivid than those of the real Richard Peyton III. Now he understood the meaning of the danger line. If the thought-intensity control was turned too high, madness would certainly result.

Peyton switched off the instrument so that he could think without interruption. He understood now what the robot had meant when it said that the other inhabitants of the city were sleeping. There were other men in Comarre, lying entranced beneath the thought projectors.

His mind went back to the long corridor and its hundreds of metal doors. On his way down he had passed through many such galleries and it was clear that the greater part of the city was no more than a vast honey-comb of chambers in which thousands of men could dream away their lives.

One after another he checked the circuits on the board. The great majority were dead, but perhaps fifty were still operating. And each of them carried all the thoughts, desires, and emotions of the human mind.

Now that he was fully conscious, Peyton could understand how he had been tricked, but the knowledge brought little consolation. He could see the flaws in these synthetic worlds, could observe how all the critical faculties of the mind were numbed while an endless stream of simple but vivid emotions was poured into it.

Yes, it all seemed very simple now. But it did not alter the fact that this artificial world was utterly real to the beholder—so real that the pain of leaving it still burned in his own mind.

For nearly an hour, Peyton explored the worlds of the fifty sleeping minds. It was a fascinating though repulsive quest. In that hour he learned more of the human brain and its hidden ways than he had ever dreamed existed. When he had finished he sat very still for a long time at the controls of the machine, analyzing his new-found knowledge. His wisdom had advanced by many years, and his youth seemed suddenly very far away.

For the first time he had direct knowledge of the fact that the perverse and evil desires that sometimes ruffled the surface of his own mind were shared by all human beings. The builders of Comarre had cared nothing for good or evil—and the machines had been their faithful servants.

It was satisfactory to know that his theories had been correct. Peyton understood now the narrowness of his escape. If he fell asleep again within these walls he might never awake. Chance had saved him once, but it would not do so again.

The thought projectors must be put out of action, so thoroughly that the robots could never repair them. Though they could handle normal breakdowns, the robots could not deal with deliberate sabotage on the scale Peyton was envisaging. When he had finished, Comarre would be a menace no longer. It would never trap his mind again, or the minds of any future visitors who might come this way.

First he would have to locate the sleepers and revive them. That might be a lengthy task, but fortunately the machine level was equipped with standard monovision search apparatus. With it he could see and hear everything in the city, simply by focusing the carrier beams on the required spot. He could even project his voice if necessary, but not his image. That type of machine had not come into general use until after the building of Comarre.

It took him a little while to master the controls, and at first the beam wandered erratically all over the city. Peyton found himself looking into any number of surprising places, and once he even got a glimpse of the forest— though it was upside down. He wondered if Leo was still around, and with some difficulty he located the entrance.

Yes, there it was, just as he had left it the day before. And a few yards away the faithful Leo was lying with his head toward the city and a distinctly worried look on his face. Peyton was deeply touched. He wondered if he could get the lion into Comarre. The moral support would be valuable, for he was beginning to feel need of companionship after the night's experiences.

Methodically he searched the wall of the city and was greatly relieved to discover several concealed entrances at ground level. He had been wondering how he was going to leave. Even if he could work the matter-transmitter in reverse, the prospect was not an attractive

one. He much preferred an old-fashioned physical movement through space.

The openings were all sealed, and for a moment he
was baffled. Then he began to search for a robot. After
some delay, he discovered one of the late A-Five's twins
rolling along a corridor on some mysterious errand. To
his relief, it obeyed his command unquestioningly and
opened the door.

Peyton drove the beam through the walls again and
brought the focus point to rest a few feet away from Leo.
Then he called, softly:

"Leo!"

The lion looked up, startled.

"Hello, Leo—it's me—Peyton!"

Looking puzzled, the lion walked slowly around in a
circle. Then it gave up and sat down helplessly.

With a great deal of persuasion, Peyton coaxed Leo
up to the entrance. The lion recognized his voice and
seemed willing to follow, but it was a sorely puzzled and
rather nervous animal. It hesitated for a moment at the
opening, liking neither Comarre nor the silently waiting
robot.

Very patiently Peyton instructed Leo to follow the
robot. He repeated his remarks in different words until
he was sure the lion understood. Then he spoke directly
to the machine and ordered it to guide the lion to the
control chamber. He watched for a moment to see that
Leo was following. Then, with a word of encouragement,
he left the strangely assorted pair.

It was rather disappointing to find that he could not see
into any of the sealed rooms behind the poppy symbol.
They were shielded from the beam or else the focusing
controls had been set so that the monovisor could not be
used to pry into that volume of space.

Peyton was not discouraged. The sleepers would wake
up the hard way, as he had done. Having looked into their

private worlds, he felt little sympathy for them and only
a sense of duty impelled him to wake them. They de-
served no consideration.

A horrible thought suddenly assailed him. What had
the projectors fed into his own mind in response to his
desires, in that forgotten idyll from which he had been so
reluctant to return? Had his own hidden thoughts been
as disreputable as those of the other dreamers?

It was an uncomfortable idea, and he put it aside as he
sat down once more at the central switchboard. First he
would disconnect the circuits, then he would sabotage the
projectors so that they could never again be used. The
spell that Comarre had cast over so many minds would
be broken forever.

Peyton reached forward to throw the multiplex circuit breakers, but he never completed the movement.
Gently but very firmly, four metal arms clasped his body
from behind. Kicking and struggling, he was lifted into
the air away from the controls and carried to the center
of the room. There he was set down again, and the
metal arms released him.

More angry than alarmed, Peyton whirled to face his
captor. Regarding him quietly from a few yards away
was the most complex robot he had ever seen. Its body
was nearly seven feet high, and rested on a dozen fat
balloon tires.

From various parts of its metal chassis, tentacles, arms,
rods, and other less easily describable mechanisms projected in all directions. In two places, groups of limbs
were busily at work dismantling or repairing pieces of
machinery which Peyton recognized with a guilty start.

Silently Peyton weighed his opponent. It was clearly a
robot of the very highest order. But it had used physical
violence against him—and no robot could do that against
a man, though it might refuse to obey his orders. Only
under the direct control of another human mind could a

robot commit such an act. So there was life, conscious and hostile life, somewhere in the city.

"Who are you?" exclaimed Peyton at last, addressing not the robot, but the controller behind it.

With no detectable time lag the machine answered in a precise and automatic voice that did not seem to be merely the amplified speech of a human being.

"I am the Engineer."

"Then come out and let me see you."

"You are seeing me."

It was the inhuman tone of the voice, as much as the words themselves, that made Peyton's anger evaporate in a moment and replaced it with a sense of unbelieving wonder.

There was no human being controlling this machine. It was as automatic as the other robots of the city—but unlike them, and all other robots the world had ever known, it had a will and a consciousness of its own.

6 ◄► THE NIGHTMARE

As Peyton stared wide-eyed at the machine before him, he felt his scalp crawling, not with fright, but with the sheer intensity of his excitement. His quest had been rewarded—the dream of nearly a thousand years was here before his eyes.

Long ago the machines had won a limited intelligence. Now at last they had reached the goal of consciousness itself. This was the secret Thordarsen would have given to the world—the secret the Council had sought to suppress for fear of the consequences it might bring.

The passionless voice spoke again.

"I am glad that you realize the truth. It will make things easier."

"You can read my mind?" gasped Peyton.

"Naturally. That was done from the moment you entered."

"Yes, I gathered that," said Peyton grimly. "And what do you intend to do with me now?"

"I must prevent you from damaging Comarre."

That, thought Peyton, was reasonable enough.

"Suppose I left now? Would that suit you?"

"Yes. That would be good."

Peyton could not help laughing. The Engineer was still a robot, in spite of all its near-humanity. It was incapable of guile, and perhaps that gave him an advantage. Somehow he must trick it into revealing its secrets. But once again the robot read his mind.

"I will not permit it. You have learned too much already. You must leave at once. I will use force if necessary."

Peyton decided to fight for time. He could, at least, discover the limits of this amazing machine's intelligence.

"Before I go, tell me this. Why are you called the Engineer?"

The robot answered readily enough.

"If serious faults developed that cannot be repaired by the robots, I deal with them. I could rebuild Comarre if necessary. Normally, when everything is functioning properly, I am quiescent."

How alien, thought Peyton, the idea of "quiescence" was to a human mind. He could not help feeling amused at the distinction the Engineer had drawn between itself and "the robots." He asked the obvious question.

"And if something goes wrong with you?"

"There are two of us. The other is quiescent now. Each can repair the other. That was necessary once, three hundred years ago."

It was a flawless system. Comarre was safe from accident for millions of years. The builders of the city had set these eternal guardians to watch over them while they went in search of their dreams. No wonder that, long after its makers had died, Comarre was still fulfilling its strange purpose.

What a tragedy it was, thought Peyton, that all this genius had been wasted! The secrets of the Engineer could revolutionize robot technology, could bring a new world into being. Now that the first conscious machines had been built, was there any limit to what lay beyond?

"No," said the Engineer unexpectedly. "Thordarsen told me that the robots would one day be more intelligent than man."

It was strange to hear the machine uttering the name of its maker. So that was Thordarsen's dream! It's full immensity had not yet dawned on him. Though he had been half-prepared for it, he could not easily accept the conclusions. After all, between the robot and the human mind lay an enormous gulf.

"No greater than that between man and the animals from which he rose, so Thordarsen once said. You, Man, are no more than a very complex robot. I am simpler, but more efficient. That is all."

Very carefully Peyton considered the statement. If indeed Man was no more than a complex robot—a machine composed of living cells rather than wires and vacuum tubes—yet more complex robots would one day be made. When that day came, the supremacy of Man would be ended. The machines might still be his servants, but they would be more intelligent than their master.

It was very quiet in the great room lined with the racks of analyzers and relay panels. The Engineer was watching Peyton intently, its arms and tentacles still busy on their repair work.

Peyton was beginning to feel desperate. Characteristically the opposition had made him more determined than ever. Somehow he must discover how the Engineer was built. Otherwise he would waste all his life trying to match the genius of Thordarsen.

It was useless. The robot was one jump ahead of him.

"You cannot make plans against me. If you do try to escape through that door, I shall throw this power unit at your legs. My probable error at this range is less than half a centimeter."

One could not hide from the thought analyzers. The plan had been scarcely half-formed in Peyton's mind, but the Engineer knew it already.

Both Peyton and the Engineer were equally surprised by the interruption. There was a sudden flash of tawny gold, and half a ton of bone and sinew, traveling at forty miles an hour, struck the robot amidships.

For a moment there was a great flailing of tentacles. Then, with a sound like the crack of doom, the Engineer lay sprawling on the floor. Leo, licking his paws thoughtfully, crouched over the fallen machine.

He could not quite understand this shining animal which had been threatening his master. Its skin was the toughest he had encountered since a very ill-advised disagreement with a rhinoceros many years ago.

"Good boy!" shouted Peyton gleefully. "Keep him down!"

The Engineer had broken some of his larger limbs, and the tentacles were too weak to do any damage. Once again Peyton found his tool kit invaluable. When he had finished, the Engineer was certainly incapable of movement, though Peyton had not touched any of the neural circuits. That, somehow, would have been rather too much like murder.

"You can get off now, Leo," he said when the task was finished. The lion obeyed with poor grace.

"I'm sorry to have to do this," said Peyton hypocritically, "but I hope you appreciate my point of view. Can you still speak?"

"Yes," replied the Engineer. "What do you intend to do now?"

Peyton smiled. Five minutes ago, he had been the one to ask the question. How long, he wondered, would it take for the Engineer's twin to arrive on the scene? Though Leo could deal with the situation if it came to a trial of strength, the other robot would have been warned and might be able to make things very unpleasant for them. It could, for instance, switch off the lights.

The glow tubes died and darkness fell. Leo gave a mournful howl of dismay. Feeling rather annoyed, Peyton drew his torch and twitched it on.

"It doesn't really make any difference to me," he said. "You might just as well switch them on again."

The Engineer said nothing. But the glow tubes lit once more.

How on earth, thought Peyton, could you fight an enemy who could read your thoughts and could even watch you preparing your defenses? He would have to avoid thinking of any idea that might react to his disadvantage, such as—he stopped himself just in time. For a moment he blocked his thoughts by trying to integrate Armstrong's omega function in his head. Then he got his mind under control again.

"Look," he said at last, "I'll make a bargain with you."

"What is that? I do not know the word."

"Never mind," Peyton replied hurriedly. "My suggestion is this. Let me waken the men who are trapped here, give me your fundamental circuits, and I'll leave without touching anything. You will have obeyed your builders' orders and no harm will have been done."

A human being might have argued over the matter, but not so the robot. Its mind took perhaps a thousandth of a second to weigh any situation, however involved.

"Very well. I see from your mind that you intend to keep the agreement. But what does the word 'blackmail' mean?"

Peyton flushed.

"It doesn't matter," he said hastily. "It's only a common human expression. I suppose your—er—colleague will be here in a moment?"

"He has been waiting outside for some time," replied the robot. "Will you keep your dog under control?"

Peyton laughed. It was too much to expect a robot to know zoology.

"Lion, then," said the robot, correcting itself as it read his mind.

Peyton addressed a few words to Leo and, to make doubly sure, wound his fingers in the lion's mane. Before he could frame the invitation with his lips, the second robot rolled silently into the room. Leo growled and tried to tug away, but Peyton calmed him.

In every respect Engineer II was a duplicate of its colleague. Even as it came toward him it dipped into his mind in the disconcerting manner that Peyton could never get used to.

"I see that you wish to go to the dreamers," it said. "Follow me."

Peyton was tired of being ordered around. Why didn't the robots ever say "please"?

"Follow me, please," repeated the machine, with the slightest possible accentuation.

Peyton followed.

Once again he found himself in the corridor with the hundreds of poppy-embossed doors—or a similar corridor. The robot led him to a door indistinguishable from the rest and came to a halt in front of it.

Silently the metal plate slid open, and, not without qualms, Peyton stepped into the darkened room.

On the couch lay a very old man. At first sight he seemed to be dead. Certainly his breathing had slowed to the point of cessation. Peyton stared at him for a moment. Then he spoke to the robot.

"Waken him."

Somewhere in the depths of the city the stream of impulses through a thought projector ceased. A universe that had never existed crumbled to ruins.

From the couch two burning eyes glowed up at Peyton, lit with the light of madness. They stared through him and beyond, and from the thin lips poured a stream of jumbled words that Peyton could barely distinguish. Over and over again the old man cried out names that must be those of people or places in the dream world from which he had been wrenched. It was at once horrible and pathetic.

"Stop it!" cried Peyton. "You are back in reality now."

The glowing eyes seemed to see him for the first time. With an immense effort the old man raised himself.

"Who are you?" he quavered. Then, before Peyton could answer, he continued in a broken voice. "This must be a nightmare—go away, go away. Let me wake up!"

Overcoming his repulsion, Peyton put his hand on the emaciated shoulder.

"Don't worry—you are awake. Don't you remember?" The other did not seem to hear him.

"Yes, it must be a nightmare—it must be! But why don't I wake up? Nyran, Cressidor, where are you? I cannot find you!"

Peyton stood it as long as he could, but nothing he did could attract the old man's attention again. Sick at heart, he turned to the robot.

"Send him back."

Slowly the raving ceased. The frail body fell back on the couch, and once again the wrinkled face became a passionless mask.

"Are they all as mad as this?" asked Peyton finally.

"But he is not mad."

"What do you mean? Of course he is!"

"He has been entranced for many years. Suppose you went to a far land and changed your mode of living completely, forgetting all you had ever known of your previous life. Eventually you would have no more knowledge of it than you have of your first childhood.

"If by some miracle you were then suddenly thrown back in time, you would behave in just that way. Remember, his dream life is completely real to him and he has lived it now for many years."

That was true enough. But how could the Engineer possess such insight? Peyton turned to it in amazement, but as usual had no need to frame the question.

"Thordarsen told me this the other day while we were still building Comarre. Even then some of the dreamers had been entranced for twenty years."

"The other day?"

"About five hundred years ago, you would call it."

The words brought a strange picture into Peyton's mind. He could visualize the lonely genius, working here among his robots, perhaps with no human companions left. All the others would long since have gone in search of their dreams.

But Thordarsen might have stayed on, the desire for

creation still linking him to the world, until he had finished his work. The two engineers, his greatest achievement and perhaps the most wonderful feat of electronics
of which the world had record, were his ultimate master-
pieces.

The waste and the pity of it overwhelmed Peyton.
More than ever he was determined that, because the
embittered genius had thrown away his life, his work
should not perish, but be given to the world.

"Will all the dreamers be like this?" he asked the robot.

"All except the newest. They may still remember their
first lives."

"Take me to one of them."

The room they entered next was identical with the
other, but the body lying on the couch was that of a man
of no more than forty.

"How long has he been here?" asked Peyton.

"He came only a few weeks ago—the first visitor we
had for many years until your coming."

"Wake him, please."

The eyes opened slowly. There was no insanity in them,
only wonder and sadness. Then came the dawn of recollection, and the man half rose to a sitting position. His
first words were completely rational.

"Why have you called me back? Who are you?"

"I have just escaped from the thought projectors," explained Peyton. "I want to release all who can be saved."

The other laughed bitterly.

"Saved! From what? It took me forty years to escape
from the world, and now you would drag me back to it!
Go away and leave me in peace!"

Peyton would not retreat so easily.

"Do you think that this make-believe world of yours is
better than reality? Have you no desire to escape from it
at all?"

Again the other laughed, with no trace of humor.

"Comarre is reality to me. The world never gave me anything, so why should I wish to return to it? I have found peace here, and that is all I need."

Quite suddenly Peyton turned on his heels and left. Behind him he heard the dreamer fall back with a contented sigh. He knew when he had been beaten. And he knew now why he had wished to revive the others.

It had not been through any sense of duty, but for his own selfish purpose. He had wished to convince himself that Comarre was evil. Now he knew that it was not. There would always be, even in Utopia, some for whom the world had nothing to offer but sorrow and disillusion.

They would be fewer and fewer with the passage of time. In the dark ages of a thousand years ago most of mankind had been misfits of some sort. However splendid the world's future, there would still be some tragedies—and why should Comarre be condemned because it offered them their only hope of peace?

He would try no more experiments. His own robust faith and confidence had been severely shaken. And the dreamers of Comarre would not thank him for his pains.

He turned to the Engineer again. The desire to leave the city had grown very intense in the last few minutes, but the most important work was still to be done. As usual, the robot forestalled him.

"I have what you want," he said. "Follow me, please."

It did not lead, as Peyton had half expected, back to the machine levels, with their maze of control equipment. When their journey had finished, they were higher than Peyton had ever been before, in a little circular room he suspected might be at the very apex of the city. There were no windows, unless the curious plates set in the wall could be made transparent by some secret means.

It was a study, and Peyton gazed at it with awe as

he realized who had worked here many centuries ago. The walls were lined with ancient textbooks that had not been disturbed for five hundred years. It seemed as if Thordarsen had left only a few hours before. There was even a half-finished circuit pinned on a drawing board against the wall.

"It almost looks as if he was interrupted," said Peyton, half to himself.

"He was," answered the robot.

"What do you mean? Didn't he join the others when he had finished you?"

It was difficult to believe that there was absolutely no emotion behind the reply, but the words were spoken in the same passionless tones as everything else the robot had ever said.

"When he had finished us, Thordarsen was still not satisfied. He was not like the others. He often told us that he had found happiness in the building of Comarre. Again and again he said that he would join the rest, but always there was some last improvement he wanted to make. So it went on until one day we found him lying here in this room. He had stopped. The word I see in your mind is 'death,' but I have no thought for that."

Peyton was silent. It seemed to him that the great scientist's ending had not been an ignoble one. The bitterness that had darkened his life had lifted from it at the last. He had known the joy of creation. Of all the artists who had come to Comarre, he was the greatest. And now his work would not be wasted.

The robot glided silently toward a steel desk, and one of its tentacles disappeared into a drawer. When it emerged it was holding a thick volume, bound between sheets of metal. Wordlessly it handed the book to Peyton, who opened it with trembling hands. It contained many thousands of pages of thin, very tough material.

Written on the flyleaf in a bold, firm hand were the words:

Rolf Thordarsen
Notes on Subelectronics
Begun: Day 2, Month 13, 2598.

Underneath was more writing, very difficult to decipher and apparently scrawled in frantic haste. As he read, understanding came at last to Peyton with the suddenness of an equatorial dawn.

To the reader of these words:

I, Rolf Thordarsen, meeting no understanding in my own age, send this message into the future. If Comarre still exists, you will have seen my handiwork and must have escaped the snares I set for lesser minds. Therefore you are fitted to take this knowledge to the world. Give it to the scientists and tell them to use it wisely.

I have broken down the barrier between Man and Machine. Now they must share the future equally.

Peyton read the message several times, his heart warming toward his long-dead ancestor. It was a brilliant scheme. In this way, as perhaps in no other, Thordarsen had been able to send his message safely down the ages, knowing that only the right hands would receive it. Peyton wondered if this had been Thordarsen's plan when he first joined the Decadents or whether he had evolved it later in his life. He would never know.

He looked again at the Engineer and thought of the world that would come when all robots had reached consciousness. Beyond that he looked still farther into the mists of the future.

The robot need have none of the limitations of Man, none of his pitiful weaknesses. It would never let passions cloud its logic, would never be swayed by self-interest and ambition. It would be complementary to man.

Peyton remembered Thordarsen's words, "Now they must share the future equally."

Peyton stopped his daydream. All this, if it ever came, might be centuries in the future. He turned to the Engineer.

"I am ready to leave. But one day I shall return."

The robot backed slowly away from him.

"Stand perfectly still," it ordered.

Peyton looked at the Engineer in puzzlement. Then he glanced hurriedly at the ceiling. There again was that enigmatic bulge under which he had found himself when he first entered the city such an age ago.

"Hey!" he cried. "I don't want—"

It was too late. Behind him was the dark screen, blacker than night itself. Before him lay the clearing, with the forest at its edge. It was evening, and the sun was nearly touching the trees.

There was a sudden whimpering noise behind him: a very frightened lion was looking out at the forest with unbelieving eyes. Leo had not enjoyed his transfer.

"It's all over now, old chap," said Peyton reassuringly. "You can't blame them for trying to get rid of us as quickly as they could. After all, we did smash up the place a bit between us. Come along—I don't want to spend the night in the forest."

On the other side of the world, a group of scientists was dispersing with what patience it could, not yet knowing the full extent of its triumph. In Central Tower, Richard Peyton II had just discovered that his son had not spent the last two days with his cousins in South America, and was composing a speech of welcome for the prodigal's return.

Far above the Earth the World Council was laying down plans soon to be swept away by the coming of the

Third Renaissance. But the cause of all the trouble knew nothing of this and, for the moment, cared less.

Slowly Peyton descended the marble steps from that mysterious doorway whose secret was still hidden from him. Leo followed a little way behind, looking over his shoulder and growling quietly now and then.

Together, they started back along the metal road, through the avenue of stunted trees. Peyton was glad that the sun had not yet set. At night this road would be glowing with its internal radioactivity, and the twisted trees would not look pleasant silhouetted against the stars.

At the bend in the road he paused for a while and looked back at the curving metal wall with its single black opening whose appearance was so deceptive. All his feeling of triumph seemed to fade away. He knew that as long as he lived he could never forget what lay behind those towering walls—the cloying promise of peace and utter contentment.

Deep in his soul he felt the fear that any satisfaction, any achievement the outer world could give might seem vain beside the effortless bliss offered by Comarre. For an instant he had a nightmare vision of himself, broken and old, returning along this road to seek oblivion. He shrugged his shoulders and put the thought aside.

Once he was out on the plain his spirits rose swiftly. He opened the precious book again and ruffled through its pages of microprint, intoxicated by the promise that it held. Ages ago the slow caravans had come this way, bearing gold and ivory for Solomon the Wise. But all their treasure was as nothing beside this single volume, and all the wisdom of Solomon could not have pictured the new civilization of which this volume was to be the seed.

Presently Peyton began to sing, something he did very seldom and extremely badly. The song was a very old one, so old that it came from an age before atomic power, before interplanetary travel, even before the coming of flight. It had to do with a certain hairdresser in Seville, wherever Seville might be.

Leo stood it in silence for as long as he could. Then he, too, joined in. The duet was not a success.

When night descended, the forest and all its secrets had fallen below the horizon. With his face to the stars and Leo watching by his side, Peyton slept well.

This time he did not dream.

Against the Fall of Night

PROLOGUE

Not once in a generation did the voice of the city change as it was changing now. Day and night, age after age, it had never faltered. To myriads of men it had been the first and the last sound they had ever heard. It was part of the city: when it ceased the city would be dead and the desert sands would be settling in the great streets of Diaspar.

Even here, half a mile above the ground, the sudden hush brought Convar out to the balcony. Far below, the moving ways were still sweeping between the great buildings, but now they were thronged with silent crowds. Something had drawn the languid people of the city from their homes: in their thousands they were drifting slowly between the cliffs of colored metal. And then Convar saw that all those myriads of faces were turned towards the sky.

For a moment fear crept into his soul—fear lest after all these ages the Invaders had come again to Earth. Then he too was staring at the sky, entranced by a wonder he had never hoped to see again. He watched for many minutes before he went to fetch his infant son.

The child Alvin was frightened at first. The soaring spires of the city, the moving specks two thousand feet below—these were part of his world, but the thing in the sky was beyond all his experience. It was larger than any of the city's buildings, and its whiteness was so dazzling that it hurt the eye. Though it seemed to be solid, the restless winds were changing its outlines even as he watched.

Once, Alvin knew, the skies of Earth had been filled with strange shapes. Out of space the great ships had come, bearing unknown treasures, to berth at the Port of Diaspar. But that was half a billion years ago: before the beginning of history the Port had been buried by the drifting sand.

Convar's voice was sad when presently he spoke to his son.

"Look at it well, Alvin," he said. "It may be the last the world will ever know. I have only seen one other in all my life, and once they filled the skies of Earth."

They watched in silence, and with them all the thousands in the streets and towers of Diaspar, until the last cloud slowly faded from sight, sucked dry by the hot, parched air of the unending deserts.

The lesson was finished. The drowsy whisper of the hyp-none rose suddenly in pitch and ceased abruptly on a thrice repeated note of command. Then the machine blurred and vanished, but still Alvin sat staring into noth-ingness while his mind slipped back through the ages to meet reality again.

Jeserac was the first to speak: his voice was worried and a little uncertain.

"Those are the oldest records in the world, Alvin—the only ones that show Earth as it was before the Invaders came. Very few people indeed have ever seen them."

Slowly the boy turned towards his tutor. There was something in his eyes that worried the old man, and once again Jeserac regretted his action. He began to talk quickly, as if trying to set his own conscience at ease.

"You know that we never talk about the ancient times, and I only showed you those records because you were so anxious to see them. Don't let them upset you: as long as we're happy, does it matter how much of the world we occupy? The people you have been watching had more space, but they were less contented than we."

Was that true? Alvin wondered. He thought once more of the desert lapping round the island that was Diaspar, and his mind returned to the world that Earth had been. He saw again the endless leagues of blue water, greater than the land itself, rolling their waves against golden shores. His ears were still ringing with the boom of break-ers stilled these thousand million years. And he remembered the forests and prairies, and the strange beasts that had once shared the world with Man.

All this was gone. Of the oceans, nothing remained but the grey deserts of salt, the winding sheets of Earth. Salt and sand, from Pole to Pole, with only the lights of Diaspar burning in the wilderness that must one day overwhelm them.

And these were the least of the things that Man had lost, for above the desolation the forgotten stars were shining still.

"Jeserac," said Alvin at last, "once I went to the Tower of Loranne. No one lives there any more, and I could look out over the desert. It was dark, and I couldn't see the ground, but the sky was full of colored lights. I watched them for a long time, but they never moved. So presently I came away. Those were the stars, weren't they?"

Jeserac was alarmed. Exactly how Alvin had got to the Tower of Loranne was a matter for further investigation. The boy's interests were becoming—dangerous.

"Those were the stars," he answered briefly. "What of them?"

"We used to visit them once, didn't we?"

A long pause. Then, "Yes."

"Why did we stop? What *were* the invaders?"

Jeserac rose to his feet. His answer echoed back through all the teachers the world had ever known.

"That's enough for one day, Alvin. Later, when you are older, I'll tell you more—but not now. You already know too much."

Alvin never asked the question again: later, he had no need, for the answer was clear. And there was so much in Diaspar to beguile the mind that for months he could forget that strange yearning he alone seemed to feel.

Diaspar was a world in itself. Here Man had gathered all his treasures, everything that had been saved from the ruin of the past. All the cities that had ever been had given something to Diaspar: even before the coming of the Invaders its name had been known on the worlds that Man had lost.

Into the building of Diaspar had gone all the skill, all the artistry of the Golden Ages. When the great days were coming to an end, men of genius had remoulded the city and given it the machines that made it immortal. Whatever might be forgotten, Diaspar would live and bear the descendants of Man safely down the stream of Time.

They were, perhaps, as contented as any race the world had known, and after their fashion they were happy. They spent their long lives amid beauty that had never been surpassed, for the labour of millions of centuries had been dedicated to the glory of Diaspar.

This was Alvin's world, a world which for ages had been sinking into a gracious decadence. Of this Alvin was still unconscious, for the present was so full of wonder that it was easy to forget the past. There was so much to do, so much to learn before the long centuries of his youth ebbed away.

Music had been the first of the arts to attract him, and for a while he had experimented with many instruments. But this most ancient of all arts was now so complex that it might take a thousand years for him to master all its secrets, and in the end he abandoned his ambitions. He could listen, but he could never create.

For a long time the thought-converter gave him great delight. On its screen he shaped endless patterns of form and color, usually copies—deliberate or otherwise—of the ancient masters. More and more frequently he found himself creating dream landscapes from the vanished Dawn World, and often his thoughts turned wistfully to the records that Jeserac had shown him. So the smouldering flame of his discontent burned slowly towards the level of consciousness, though as yet he was scarcely worried by the vague restlessness he often felt.

But through the months and the years, that restlessness was growing. Once Alvin had been content to share the pleasures and interests of Diaspar, but now he knew that they were not sufficient. His horizons were expanding, and the knowledge that all his life must be bounded by the walls of the city was becoming intolerable to him. Yet he knew well enough that there was no alternative, for the wastes of the desert covered all the world.

He had seen the desert only a few times in his life, but he knew no one else who had ever seen it at all. His people's fear of the outer world was something he could not understand: to him it held no terror, but only mystery. When he was weary of Diaspar, it called to him as it was calling now.

The moving ways were glittering with life and color as the people of the city went about their affairs. They smiled at Alvin as he worked his way to the central high-speed action. Sometimes they greeted him by name: once it had been flattering to think that he was known to the whole of Diaspar, but now it gave him little pleasure.

In minutes the express channel had swept him away from the crowded heart of the city, and there were few people in sight when it came to a smooth halt against a long platform of brightly colored marble. The moving ways were so much a part of his life that Alvin had never imagined any other form of transport. An engineer of the ancient world would have gone slowly mad trying to understand how a solid roadway could be fixed at both ends while its center travelled at a hundred miles an hour. One day Alvin might be puzzled too, but for the present he accepted his environment as uncritically as all the other citizens of Diaspar.

This area of the city was almost deserted. Although the population of Diaspar had not altered for millennia, it was the custom for families to move at frequent intervals. One day the tide of life would sweep this way again, but the great towers had been lonely now for a hundred thousand years.

The marble platform ended against a wall pierced with brilliantly lighted tunnels. Alvin selected one without hesitation and stepped into it. The peristaltic field seized him at once, and propelled him forward while he lay back luxuriously, watching his surroundings.

It no longer seemed possible that he was in a tunnel far underground. The art that had used all Diaspar for its canvas had been busy here, and above Alvin the skies seemed open to the winds of heaven. All around were the spires of the city, gleaming in the sunlight. It was not the city as he knew it, but the Diaspar of a much earlier age. Although most of the great buildings were familiar, there were subtle differences that added to the interest of the scene. Alvin wished he could linger, but he had never found any way of retarding his progress through the tunnel.

All too soon he was gently set down in a large elliptical chamber, completely surrounded by windows. Through these he could catch tantalizing glimpses of gardens ablaze with brilliant flowers. There were gardens still in Diaspar, but these had existed only in the mind of the artist who conceived them. Certainly there were no such flowers as these in the world today.

Alvin stepped through one of the windows—and the illusion was shattered. He was in a circular passageway curving steeply upwards. Beneath his feet the floor began to creep slowly forward, as if eager to lead him to his goal. He walked a few paces until his speed was so great that further effort would be wasted.

The corridor still inclined upwards, and in a few hundred feet had curved through a complete right angle. But only logic knew this: to the senses it was now as if one were being hurried along an absolutely level corridor. The fact that he was in reality travelling up a vertical shaft thousands of feet deep gave Alvin no sense of insecurity, for a failure of the polarizing field was unthinkable.

Presently the corridor began to slope "downwards" again until once more it had turned through a right angle. The movement of the floor slowed imperceptibly until it came to rest at the end of a long hall lined with mirrors. Alvin was now, he knew, almost at the summit of the Tower of Loranne.

He lingered for a while in the hall of mirrors, for it had a fascination that was unique. There was nothing like it, as far as Alvin knew, in the rest of Diaspar. Through some whim of the artist, only a few of the mirrors reflected the scene as it really was—and even those, Alvin was convinced, were constantly changing their position. The rest certainly reflected *something*, but it was faintly disconcerting to see oneself walking amid ever-changing and quite imaginary surroundings. Alvin wondered what he would do if he saw anyone else approaching him in the mirror-world, but so far the situation had never arisen.

Five minutes later he was in a small, bare room through which a warm wind blew continually. It was part of the tower's ventilating system, and the moving air escaped through a series of wide openings that pierced the wall of the building. Through them one could get a glimpse of the world beyond Diaspar.

It was perhaps too much to say that Diaspar had been deliberately built so that its inhabitants could see nothing of the outer world. Yet it was strange that from nowhere else in the city, as far as Alvin knew, could one see the desert. The outermost towers of Diaspar formed a wall around the city, turning their backs upon the hostile world beyond, and Alvin thought again of his people's strange reluctance to speak or even to think of anything outside their little universe.

Thousands of feet below, the sunlight was taking leave of the desert. The almost horizontal rays made a pattern of light against the eastern wall of the little room, and Alvin's own shadow loomed enormous behind him. He shaded his eyes against the glare and peered down at the land upon which no man had walked for unknown ages.

There was little to see: only the long shadows of the sand dunes and, far to the west, the low range of broken hills beyond which the sun was setting. It was strange to think that of all the millions of living men, he alone had seen this sight.

There was no twilight: with the going of the sun, night swept like a wind across the desert, scattering the stars before it. High in the south burned a strange formation that had puzzled Alvin before—a perfect circle of six colored stars, with a single white giant at its center. Few other stars had such brilliance, for the great suns that had once burned so fiercely in the glory of youth were now guttering to their doom.

For a long time Alvin knelt at the opening, watching the stars fall towards the west. Here in the glimmering darkness, high above the city, his mind seemed to be working with a supernormal clarity. There were still tremendous gaps in his knowledge, but slowly the problem of Diaspar was beginning to reveal itself.

The human race had changed—and he had not. Once, the curiosity and the desire for knowledge which cut him off from the rest of his people had been shared by all the world. Far back in time, millions of years ago, something must have happened that had changed mankind completely. Those unexplained references to the Invaders—did the answer lie there?

It was time he returned. As he rose to leave, Alvin was suddenly struck by a thought that had never occurred to him before. The air vent was almost horizontal, and perhaps a dozen feet long. He had always imagined that it ended in the sheer wall of the tower, but this was a pure assumption. There were, he realized now, several other possibilities. Indeed, it was more than likely that there would be a ledge of some kind beneath the opening, if only for reasons of safety. It was too late to do any exploring now, but tomorrow he would come again. . . .

He was sorry to have to lie to Jeserac, but if the old man disapproved of his eccentricities it was only kindness to conceal the truth. Exactly what he hoped to discover, Alvin could not have said. He knew perfectly well that if by any means he succeeded in leaving Diaspar, he would soon have to return. But the schoolboy excitement of a possible adventure was its own justification.

It was not difficult to work his way along the tunnel, though he could not have done it easily a year before. The thought of a sheer five-thousand-foot drop at the end worried Alvin not at all, for Man had completely lost his fear of heights. And, in fact, the drop was only a matter of a yard onto a wide terrace running right and left athwart the face of the tower.

Alvin scrambled out into the open, the blood pounding in his veins. Before him, no longer framed in a narrow rectangle of stone, lay the whole expanse of the desert. Above, the face of the tower still soared hundreds of feet into the sky. The neighboring buildings stretched away to north and south, an avenue of titans. The Tower of Loranne, Alvin noted with interest, was not the only one with air vents opening towards the desert. For a moment he stood drinking in the tremendous landscape: then he began to examine the ledge on which he was standing.

It was perhaps twenty feet wide, and ended abruptly in a sheer drop to the ground. Alvin, gazing fearlessly over the edge of the precipice, judged that the desert was at least a mile below. There was no hope in that direction.

Far more interesting was the fact that a flight of steps led down from one end of the terrace, apparently to another ledge a few hundred feet below. The steps were cut in the sheer face of the building, and Alvin wondered if they led all the way to the surface. It was an exciting possibility: in his enthusiasm, he overlooked the physical implications of a five-thousand-foot descent.

But the stairway was little more than a hundred feet long. It came to a sudden end against a great block of stone that seemed to have been welded across it. There was no way past: deliberately and thoroughly, the route had been barred.

Alvin approached the obstacle with a sinking heart. He had forgotten the sheer impossibility of climbing a stairway a mile high, if indeed he could have completed the descent, and he felt a baffled annoyance at having come so far only to meet with failure.

He reached the stone, and for the first time saw the message engraved upon it. The letters were archaic, but he could decipher them easily enough. Three times he read the simple inscription: then he sat down on the great stone slabs and gazed at the inaccessible land below.

THERE IS A BETTER WAY.
GIVE MY GREETINGS TO THE KEEPER OF THE RECORDS.

Alaine of Lyndar

Rorden, Keeper of the Records, concealed his surprise when his visitor announced himself. He recognized Alvin at once, and even as the boy was entering had punched out his name on the information machine. Three seconds later, Alvin's personal card was lying in his hand.

According to Jeserac, the duties of the Keeper of the Records were somewhat obscure, but Alvin had expected to find him in the heart of an enormous filing system. He had also—for no reason at all—expected to meet someone quite as old as Jeserac. Instead, he found a middle-aged man in a single room containing perhaps a dozen large machines. Apart from a few papers strewn across the desk, Rorden's greeting was somewhat absent-minded, for he was surreptitiously studying Alvin's card.

"Alaine of Lyndar?" he said. "No, I've never heard of him. But we can soon find who he was."

Alvin watched with interest while he punched a set of keys on one of the machines. Almost immediately there came the glow of a synthesizer field, and a slip of paper materialized.

"Alaine seems to have been a predecessor of mine—a *very* long time ago. I thought I knew all the Keepers for the last hundred million years, but he must have been before that. It's so long ago that only his name has been recorded, with no other details at all. Where was that inscription?"

"In the Tower of Loranne," said Alvin after a moment's hesitation.

Another set of keys was punched, but this time the field did not reappear and no paper materialized.

"What are you doing?" asked Alvin. "Where *are* all your records?"

The Keeper laughed.

"That always puzzles people. It would be impossible to keep written records of all the information we need: it's recorded electrically and automatically erased after a certain time, unless there's a special reason for preserving it. If Alaine left any message for posterity, we'll soon discover it."

"How?"

"There's no one in the world who could tell you that. All I know is that this machine is an Associator. If you give it a set of facts, it will hunt through the sum total of human knowledge until it correlates them."

"Doesn't that take a lot of time?"

"Very often. I have sometimes had to wait twenty years for an answer. So won't you sit down?" he added, the crinkles round his eyes belying his solemn voice.

Alvin had never met anyone quite like the Keeper of the Records, and he decided that he liked him. He was tired of being reminded that he was a boy, and it was pleasant to be treated as a real person.

Once again the synthesizer field flickered, and Rorden bent down to read the slip. The message must have been a long one, for it took him several minutes to finish it. Finally he sat down on one of the room's couches, looking at his visitor with eyes which, as Alvin noticed for the first time, were of a most disconcerting shrewdness.

"What does it say?" he burst out at last, unable to contain his curiosity any longer.

Rorden did not reply. Instead, he was the one to ask for information.

"Why do you want to leave Diaspar?" he said quietly. If Jeserac or his father had asked him that question,

Alvin would have found himself floundering in a morass of half-truths or downright lies. But with this man, whom he had met for only a few minutes, there seemed none of the barriers that had cut him off from those he had known all his life.

"I'm not sure," he said, speaking slowly but readily. "I've always felt like this. There's nothing outside Diaspar, I know—but I want to go there all the same."

He looked shyly at Rorden, as if expecting encouragement, but the Keeper's eyes were far away. When at last he again turned to Alvin, there was an expression on his face that the boy could not fully understand, but it held a tinge of sadness that was somewhat disturbing.

No one could have told that Rorden had come to the greatest crisis in his life. For thousands of years he had carried out his duties as the interpreter of the machines, duties requiring little initiative or enterprise. Somewhat apart from the tumult of the city, rather aloof from his fellows, Rorden had lived a happy and contented life. And now this boy had come, disturbing the ghosts of an age that had been dead for millions of centuries, and threatening to shatter his cherished peace of mind.

A few words of discouragement would be enough to destroy the threat, but looking into the anxious, unhappy eyes, Rorden knew that he could never take the easy way. Even without the message from Alaine, his conscience would have forbidden it.

"Alvin," he began, "I know there are many things that have been puzzling you. Most of all, I expect, you have wondered why we now live here in Diaspar when once the whole world was not enough for us."

Alvin nodded, wondering how the other could have read his mind so accurately.

"Well, I'm afraid I cannot answer that question completely. Don't look so disappointed: I haven't finished yet. It all started when Man was fighting the Invaders—whoever or whatever they were. Before that, he had been expanding through the stars, but he was driven back to Earth in wars of which we have no conception. Perhaps that defeat changed his character, and made him content to pass the rest of his existence on Earth. Or perhaps the Invaders promised to leave him in peace if he would remain on his own planet: we don't know. All that is certain is that he started to develop an intensely centralized culture, of which Diaspar was the final expression.

"At first there were many of the great cities, but in the end Diaspar absorbed them all, for there seems to be some force driving men together as once it drove them to the stars. Few people ever recognize its presence, but we all have a fear of the outer world, and a longing for what is known and understood. That fear may be irrational, or it may have some foundation in history, but it is one of the strongest forces in our lives."

"Then why don't I feel that way?"

"You mean that the thought of leaving Diaspar, where you have everything you need and are among all your friends, doesn't fill you with something like horror?"

"No."

The Keeper smiled wryly.

"I'm afraid I cannot say the same. But at least I can appreciate your point of view, even if I cannot share it. Once I might have felt doubtful about helping you, but not now that I've seen Alaine's message."

"You still haven't told me what it was!"

Rorden laughed.

"I don't intend to do so until you're a good deal older. But I'll tell you what it was about.

"Alaine foresaw that people like you would be born in future ages: he realized that they might attempt to leave Diaspar and he set out to help them. I imagine that whatever way you tried to leave the city, you would meet an inscription directing you to the Keeper of the Records. Knowing that the Keeper would then question his machines, Alaine left a message, buried safely among the thousands and millions of records that exist. It could only be found if the Associator was deliberately looking for it. That message directs any Keeper to assist the enquirer, *even if he disapproves of his quest.* Alaine believed that the human race was becoming decadent, and he wanted to help anyone who might regenerate it. Do you follow all this?"

Alvin nodded gravely and Rorden continued.

"I hope he was wrong. I don't believe that humanity is decadent—it's simply altered. You, of course, will agree with Alaine—but don't do so simply because you think it's fine to be different from everyone else! We are happy: if we have lost anything, we're not aware of it.

"Alaine wrote a good deal in his message, but the important part is this. *There are three ways out of Diaspar.* He does not say where they lead, nor does he give any clues as to how they can be found, though there are some very obscure references I'll have to think about. But even if what he says is true, you are far too young to leave the city. Tomorrow I must speak to your people. No, I won't give you away! But leave me now—I have a good deal to think about."

Rorden felt a little embarrassed by the boy's gratitude. When Alvin had gone, he sat for a while wondering if, after all, he had acted rightly.

There was no doubt that the boy was an atavism—a throwback to the great ages. Every few generations there still appeared minds that were the equal of any the ancient days had known. Born out of their time, they could have little influence on the peacefully dreaming world of Diaspar. The long, slow decline of the human will was too far advanced to be checked by an individual genius, however brilliant. After a few centuries of restlessness, the variants accepted their fate and ceased to struggle against it. When Alvin understood his position, would he too realize that his only hope of happiness lay in conforming with the world? Rorden wondered if, after all, it might not have been kinder in the long run to discourage him. But it was too late now: Alaine had seen to that.

The ancient Keeper of the Records must have been a remarkable man, perhaps an atavism himself. How many times down the ages had other Keepers read that message of his and acted upon it for better or worse? Surely, if there had been any earlier cases, some record would have been made.

Rorden thought intently for a moment: then, slowly at first, but soon with mounting confidence, he began to put question after question to the machines, until every Associator in the room was running at full capacity. By means now beyond the understanding of man, billions upon billions of facts were racing through the scrutinizers. There was nothing to do but wait. . . .

In after years, Alvin was often to marvel at his good fortune. Had the Keeper of the Records been unfriendly, his quest could never have begun. But Rorden, in spite of the years between them, shared something of his own curiosity. In Rorden's case, there was only the desire to uncover lost knowledge: he would never have used it, for he shared with the rest of Diaspar that dread of the outer world which Alvin found so strange. Close though their friendship became, that barrier was always to lie between them.

Alvin's life was now divided into two quite distinct portions. He continued his studies with Jeserac, acquiring the immense and intricate knowledge of people, places and customs without which no one could play any part in the life of the city. Jeserac was a conscientious but a leisurely tutor, and with so many centuries before him he felt no urgency in completing his task. He was, in fact, rather pleased that Alvin should have made friends with Rorden. The Keeper of the Records was regarded with some awe by the rest of Diaspar, for he alone had direct access to all the knowledge of the past.

How enormous and yet how incomplete that knowledge was, Alvin was slowly learning. In spite of the self-cancelling circuits which obliterated all information as soon as it was obsolete, the main registers contained a hundred trillion facts at the smallest estimate. Whether there was any limit to the capacity of the machines, Rorden did not know: that knowledge was lost with the secret of their operation.

The Associators were a source of endless wonder to Alvin, who would spend hours setting up questions of their keyboards. It was amusing to discover that people whose names began with "S" had a tendency to live in the eastern part of the city—though the machines hastened to add that the fact had no statistical significance. Alvin quickly accumulated a vast array of similar useless facts which he employed to impress his friends. At the same time, under Rorden's guidance, he was learning all that was known of the Dawn Ages, for Rorden had insisted that it would need years of preparation before he could begin his quest. Alvin had recognized the truth of this, though he sometimes rebelled against it. But after a single attempt, he abandoned any hope of acquiring knowledge prematurely.

He had been alone one day when Rorden was paying one of his rare visits to the administrative center of the city. The temptation had been too strong, and he had ordered the Associators to hunt for Alaine's message.

When Rorden returned, he found a very scared boy trying to discover why all the machines were paralyzed. To Alvin's immense relief, Rorden had only laughed and punched a series of combinations that had cleared the jam. Then he turned to culprit and tried to address him severely.

"Let that be a lesson to you, Alvin! I expected something like this, so I've blocked all the circuits I don't want you to explore. That block will remain until I think it's safe to lift it."

Alvin grinned sheepishly and said nothing. Thereafter he made no more excursions into forbidden realms.

Not for three years did Rorden make more than casual references to the purpose of their work. The time had passed quickly enough, for there was so much to learn and the knowledge that his goal was not unattainable gave Alvin patience. Then, one day when they were struggling to reconcile two conflicting maps of the ancient world, the main Associator suddenly began to call for attention.

Rorden hurried to the machine and returned with a long sheet of paper covered with writing. He ran through it quickly and looked at Alvin with a smile.

"We will soon know if the first way is still open," he said quietly.

Alvin jumped from his chair, scattering maps in all directions.

"Where is it?" he cried eagerly.

Rorden laughed and pushed him back into his seat.

"I haven't kept you waiting all this time because I wanted to," he said. "It's true that you were too young to leave Diaspar before, even if we knew how it could be done. But that's not the only reason why you had to wait. The day you came to see me, I set the machines searching through the records to discover if anyone after Alaine's time had tried to leave the city. I thought you might not be the first, and I was right. There have been many others: the last was about fifteen million years ago. They've all been very careful to leave us no clues, and I can see Alaine's influence there. In his message he stressed that only those who searched for themselves should be

allowed to find the way, so I've had to explore many blind
avenues. I knew that the secret had been hidden carefully
—yet not so carefully that it couldn't be found.

"About a year ago I began to concentrate on the idea
of transport. It was obvious that Diaspar must have had
many links with the rest of the world, and although the
Port itself has been buried by the desert for ages, I thought
that there might be other means of travel. Right at the
beginning I found that the Associators would not answer direct questions: Alaine must have put a block on
them just as I once did for your benefit. Unfortunately I
can't remove Alaine's block, so I've had to use indirect
methods.

"If there was an external transport system, there's certainly no trace of it now. Therefore, if it existed at all, it
has been deliberately concealed. I set the Associators to
investigate all the major engineering operations carried
out in the city since the records began. This is a report on
the construction of the central park—*and Alaine has
added a note to it himself*. As soon as it encountered his
name, of course, the machine knew it had finished the
search and called for me."

Rorden glanced at the paper as if rereading part of it
again. Then he continued:—

"We've always taken it for granted that all the moving
ways should converge on the Park: it seems natural for
them to do so. But this report states that the Park was
built *after* the founding of the city—many millions of
years later, in fact. *Therefore the moving ways once led
to something else.*"

"An airport, perhaps?"

"No: flying was never allowed over any city, except in
very ancient times, before the moving ways were built.
Even Diaspar is not as old as that! But listen to Alaine's
note:—

"'When the desert buried the Port of Diaspar, the

emergency system which had been built against that day was able to carry the remaining transport. It was finally closed down by Yarlan Zey, builder of the Park, having remained almost unused since the Migration.'"

Alvin looked rather puzzled.

"It doesn't tell me a great deal," he complained.

Rorden smiled. "You've been letting the Associators do too much thinking for you," he admonished gently. "Like all of Alaine's statements, it's deliberately obscure lest the wrong people should learn from it. But I think it tells us quite enough. Doesn't the name 'Yarlan Zey' mean anything to you?"

"I think I understand," said Alvin slowly. "You're talking about the Monument?"

"Yes: it's in the exact center of the Park. If you extended the moving ways, they would all meet there. *Perhaps, once upon a time, they did.*"

Alvin was already on his feet.

"Let's go and have a look," he exclaimed.

Rorden shook his head.

"You've seen the Tomb of Yarlan Zey a score of times and noticed nothing unusual about it. Before we rush off, don't you think it would be a good idea to question the machines again?"

Alvin was forced to agree, and while they were waiting began to read the report that the Associator had already produced.

"Rorden," he said at last, "what did Alaine mean when he spoke about the Migration?"

"It's a term often used in the very earliest records," answered Rorden. "It refers to the time when the other cities were decaying and all the human race was moving towards Diaspar."

"Then this 'emergency system,' whatever it is, leads to them?"

"Almost certainly."

Alvin meditated for a while.

"So you think that even if we do find the system, it will only lead to a lot of ruined cities?"

"I doubt if it will even do that," replied Rorden. "When they were abandoned, the machines were closed down and the desert will have covered them by now."

Alvin refused to be discouraged.

"But Alaine must have known that!" he protested. Rorden shrugged his shoulders.

"We're only guessing," he said, "and the Associator hasn't any information at the moment. It may take several hours, but with such a restricted subject we should have all the recorded facts before the end of the day. We'll follow your advice after all."

The screens of the city were down and the sun was shining fiercely, though its rays would have felt strangely weak to a man of the Dawn Ages. Alvin had made this journey a hundred times before, yet now it seemed almost a new adventure. When they came to the end of the moving way, he bent down and examined the surface that had carried them through the city. For the first time in his life, he began to realize something of its wonder. Here it was motionless, yet a hundred yards away it was rushing directly towards him faster than a man could run.

Rorden was watching him, but he misunderstood the boy's curiosity.

"When the Park was built," he said, "I suppose they had to remove the last section of the way. I doubt if you'll learn anything from it."

"I wasn't thinking of that," said Alvin. "I was wondering how the moving ways work."

Rorden looked astonished, for the thought had never occurred to him. Ever since man had lived in cities, they had accepted without thinking the multitudinous services that lay beneath their feet. And when the cities had become completely automatic, they had ceased even to notice that they were there.

"Don't worry about *that*," he said. "I can show you a thousand greater puzzles. Tell me how my Recorders get their information, for example."

So, without a second thought, Rorden dismissed the moving ways—one of the greatest triumphs of human engineering. The long ages of research that had gone to the making of anisotropic matter meant nothing to him. Had he been told that a substance could have the properties of a solid in one dimension and of a liquid in the other two, he would not even have registered surprise.

The Park was almost three miles across, and since every pathway was a curve of some kind all distances were considerably exaggerated. When he had been younger Alvin had spent a great deal of time among the trees and plants of this largest of the city's open spaces. He had explored the whole of it at one time or another, but in later years much of its charm had vanished. Now he understood why: he had seen the ancient records and knew that the Park was only a pale shadow of a beauty that had vanished from the world.

They met many people as they walked through the avenues of ageless trees and over the dwarf perennial grass that never needed trimming. After a while they grew tired of acknowledging greetings, for everyone knew Alvin and almost everyone knew the Keeper of the Records. So they left the paths and wandered through quiet byways almost overshadowed by trees. Sometimes the trunks crowded so closely round them that the great towers of the city were hidden from sight, and for a little while Alvin could imagine he was in the ancient world of which he had so often dreamed.

The Tomb of Yarlan Zey was the only building in the Park. An avenue of the eternal trees led up the low hill on which it stood, its rose-pink columns gleaming in the sunlight. The roof was open to the sky, and the single chamber was paved with great slabs of apparently natural stone. But for geological ages human feet had crossed and recrossed that floor and left no trace upon its inconceivably stubborn material. Alvin and Rorden walked slowly into the chamber, until they came face to face with the statue of Yarlan Zey.

The creator of the great Park sat with slightly downcast eyes, as if examining the plans spread across his knees. His face wore that curiously elusive expression that had baffled the world for so many generations. Some had dismissed it as no more than a whim of the artist's, but to others it seemed that Yarlan Zey was smiling at some secret jest. Now Alvin knew that they had been correct.

Rorden was standing motionless before the statue, as if seeing it for the first time in life. Presently he walked back a few yards and began to examine the great flagstones.

"What are you doing?" asked Alvin.

"Employing a little logic and a great deal of intuition," replied Rorden. He refused to say any more, and Alvin resumed his examination of the statue. He was still doing this when a faint sound behind him attracted his attention. Rorden, his face wreathed in smiles, was slowly sinking into the floor. He began to laugh at the boy's expression.

"I think I know how to reverse this," he said as he disappeared. "If I don't come up immediately, you'll have to pull me out with a gravity polarizer. But I don't think it will be necessary."

The last words were muffled, and, rushing to the edge of the rectangular pit, Alvin saw that his friend was already many feet below the surface. Even as he watched, the shaft deepened swiftly until Rorden had dwindled to a speck no longer recognizable as a human being. Then, to Alvin's relief, the far-off rectangle of light began to expand and the pit shortened until Rorden was standing beside him once more.

For a moment there was a profound silence. Then Rorden smiled and began to speak.

"Logic," he said, "can do wonders if it has something to work upon. This building is so simple that it couldn't conceal anything, and the only possible secret exit must be through the floor. I argued that it would be marked in some way, so I searched until I found a slab that differed from all the rest."

Alvin bent down and examined the floor.

"But it's just the same as all the others!" he protested.

Rorden put his hands on the boy's shoulders and turned him round until he was looking towards the statue. For a moment Alvin stared at it intently. Then he slowly nodded his head.

"I see," he whispered. "So *that* is the secret of Yarlan Zey!"

The eyes of the statue were fixed upon the floor at his feet. There was no mistake. Alvin moved to the next slab, and found that Yarlan Zey was no longer looking towards him.

"Not one person in a thousand would ever notice that unless they were looking for it," said Rorden, "and even then, it would mean nothing to them. At first I felt rather foolish myself, standing on that slab and going through different combinations of control thoughts. Luckily the circuits must be fairly tolerant, and the code thought turned out to be 'Alaine of Lyndar.' I tried 'Yarlan Zey' at first, but it wouldn't work, as I might have guessed. Too many people would have operated the machine by accident if that trigger thought had been used."

"It sounds very simple," admitted Alvin, "but I don't think I would have found it in a thousand years. Is that how the Associators work?"

Rorden laughed.

"Perhaps," he said. "I sometimes reach the answer before they do, but they *always* reach it." He paused for a moment. "We'll have to leave the shaft open: no one is likely to fall down it."

As they sank smoothly into the earth, the rectangle of sky dwindled until it seemed very small and far away. The shaft was lit by a phosphorescence that was part of the walls, and seemed to be at least a thousand feet deep. The walls were perfectly smooth and gave no indication of the machinery that had lowered them.

The doorway at the bottom of the shaft opened automatically as they stepped towards it. A few paces took them through the short corridor—and then they were standing, overawed by its immensity, in a great circular cavern whose walls came together in a graceful, sweeping curve three hundred feet above their heads. The column against which they were standing seemed too slender to support the hundreds of feet of rock above it. Then Alvin noticed that it did not seem an integral part of the chamber at all, but was clearly of much later construction. Rorden had come to the same conclusion.

"This column," he said, "was built simply to house the shaft down which we came. We were right about the moving ways—they all lead into this place."

Alvin had noticed, without realizing what they were, the great tunnels that pierced the circumference of the chamber. He could see that they sloped gently upwards, and now he recognized the familiar grey surface of the moving ways. Here, far beneath the heart of the city, converged the wonderful transport system that carried all the traffic of Diaspar. But these were only the severed stumps of the great roadways: the strange material that gave them life was now frozen into immobility.

Alvin began to walk towards the nearest of the tunnels. He had gone only a few paces when he realized that something was happening to the ground beneath his feet. *It was becoming transparent.* A few more yards, and he seemed to be standing in mid-air without any visible support. He stopped and stared down into the void beneath.

"Rorden!" he called. "Come and look at this!"

The other joined him, and together they gazed at the marvel beneath their feet. Faintly visible, at an indefinite depth, lay an enormous map—a great network of lines converging towards a spot beneath the central shaft. At first it seemed a confused maze, but after a while Alvin was able to grasp its main outlines. As usual, he had scarcely begun his own analysis before Rorden had finished his.

"The whole of this floor must have been transparent once," said the Keeper of the Records. "When this chamber was sealed and the shaft built, the engineers must have done something to make the center opaque. Do you understand what it is, Alvin?"

"I think so," replied the boy. "It's a map of the transport system, and those little circles must be the other cities of Earth. I can just see names beside them, but they're too faint to read."

"There must have been some form of internal illumination once," said Rorden absently. He was looking towards the walls of the chamber.

"I thought so!" he exclaimed. "Do you see how all these radiating lines lead towards the small tunnels?"

Alvin had noticed that besides the great arches of the moving ways there were innumerable smaller tunnels leading out of the chamber—tunnels that sloped downwards instead of up.

Rorden continued without waiting for a reply.

"It was a magnificent system. People would come down the moving ways, select the place they wished to visit, and then follow the appropriate line on the map."

"And what happens then?" said Alvin.

As usual, Rorden refused to speculate.

"I haven't enough information," he answered. "I wish we could read the names of those cities!" he complained, changing the subject abruptly.

Alvin had wandered away and was circumnavigating the central pillar. Presently his voice came to Rorden, slightly muffled and overlaid with echoes from the walls of the chamber.

"What is it?" called Rorden, not wishing to move, because he had nearly deciphered one of the dimly visible groups of characters. But Alvin's voice was insistent, so he went to join him.

Far beneath was the other half of the great map, its faint webwork radiating towards the points of the compass. But this time not all of it was too dim to be clearly seen, for one of the lines, and one only, was brilliantly illuminated. It seemed to have no connection with the rest of the system, and pointed like a gleaming arrow to one of the downward-sloping tunnels. Near its end the line transfixed a circle of golden light, and against that circle was the single word "LYS." That was all.

For a long time Alvin and Rorden stood gazing down at that silent symbol. To Rorden it was no more than another question for his machines, but to Alvin its promise was boundless. He tried to imagine this great chamber as it had been in the ancient days, when air transport had come to an end but the cities of Earth still had commerce one with the other. He thought of the countless millions of years that had passed with the traffic steadily dwindling and the lights on the great map dying one by one, until at last only this single line remained. He wondered how long it had gleamed there among its darkened companions, waiting to guide the steps that never came, until at last Yarlan Zey had sealed the moving ways and closed Diaspar against the world.

That had been hundreds of millions of years ago. Even then, Lys must have lost touch with Diaspar. It seemed impossible that it could have survived: perhaps, after all, the map meant nothing now.

Rorden broke into his reverie at last. He seemed a little nervous and ill at ease.

"It's time we went back," he said. "I don't think we should go any further now."

Alvin recognized the undertones in his friend's voice, and did not argue with him. He was eager to go forward, but realized that it might not be wise without further preparation. Reluctantly he turned again toward the central pillar. As he walked to the opening of the shaft, the floor beneath him gradually clouded into opacity, and the gleaming enigma far below slowly faded from sight.

Now that the way lay open at last before him, Alvin felt a strange reluctance to leave the familiar world of Diaspar. He began to discover that he himself was not immune from the fears he had so often derided in others.

Once or twice Rorden had tried to dissuade him, but the attempt had been halfhearted. It would have seemed strange to a man of the Dawn Ages that neither Alvin nor Rorden saw any danger in what they were doing. For millions of years the world had held nothing that could threaten man, and even Alvin could not imagine types of human beings greatly different from those he knew in Diaspar. That he might be detained against his will was a thought wholly inconceivable to him. At the worst, he could only fail to discover anything.

Three days later, they stood once more in the deserted chamber of the moving ways. Beneath their feet the arrow of light still pointed to Lys—and now they were ready to follow it.

As they stepped into the tunnel, they felt the familiar tug of the peristaltic field and in a moment were being swept effortlessly into the depths. The journey lasted scarcely half a minute: when it ended they were standing at one end of a long, narrow chamber in the form of a half-cylinder. At the far end, two dimly lit tunnels stretched away towards infinity.

Men of almost every civilization that had existed since the Dawn would have found their surroundings completely familiar: yet to Alvin and Rorden they were a glimpse of another world. The purpose of the long,

streamlined machine that lay aimed like a projectile at
the far tunnel was obvious, but that made it none the less
novel. Its upper portion was transparent, and looking
through the walls Alvin could see rows of luxuriously
appointed seats. There was no sign of any entrance, and
the whole machine was floating about a foot above a
single metal rod that stretched away into the distance,
disappearing in one of the tunnels. A few yards away
another rod led to the second tunnel, but no machine
floated above it. Alvin knew, as surely as if he had been
told, that somewhere beneath unknown, far-off Lys, that
second machine was waiting in another such chamber as
this.

"Well," said Rorden, rather lamely, "are you ready?"

Alvin nodded.

"I wish you'd come," he said—and at once regretted it
when he saw the disquiet on the other's face. Rorden
was the closest friend he had ever possessed, but he could
never break through the barriers that surrounded all his
race.

"I'll be back within six hours," Alvin promised, speaking
with difficulty, for there was a mysterious tightness in his
throat. "Don't bother to wait for me. If I get back early
I'll call you—there must be some communicators around
here."

It was all very casual and matter-of-fact, Alvin told
himself. Yet he could not help jumping when the walls
of the machine faded and the beautifully designed interior lay open before his eyes.

Rorden was speaking, rather quickly and jerkily.

"You'll have no difficulty in controlling the machine,"
he said. "Did you see how it obeyed that thought of mine?
I should get inside quickly in case the time delay is
fixed."

Alvin stepped aboard, placing his belongings on the
nearest seat. He turned to face Rorden, who was standing

in the barely visible frame of the doorway. For a moment there was a strained silence while each waited for the other to speak.

The decision was made for them. There was a faint flicker of translucence, and the walls of the machine had closed again. Even as Rorden began to wave farewell, the long cylinder started to ease itself forward. Before it had entered the tunnel, it was already moving faster than a man could run.

Slowly Rorden made his way back to the chamber of the moving ways with its great central pillar. Sunlight was streaming down the open shaft as he rose to the surface. When he emerged again into the Tomb of Yarlan Zey, he was disconcerted, though not surprised, to find a group of curious onlookers gathered around him.

"There's no need to be alarmed," he said gravely. "Someone has to do this every few thousand years, though it hardly seems necessary. The foundations of the city are perfectly stable—they haven't shifted a micron since the Park was built."

He walked briskly away, and as he left the tomb a quick backward glance showed him that the spectators were already dispersing. Rorden knew his fellow citizens well enough to be sure that they would think no more about the incident.

Alvin settled back on the upholstery and let his eyes wander round the interior of the machine. For the first time he noticed the indicator board that formed part of the forward wall. It carried the simple message:—

LYS

35 MINUTES

Even as he watched, the number changed to "34." That at least was useful information, though because he had no idea of the machine's speed it told him nothing about the length of the journey. The walls of the tunnel were one continual blur of grey, and the only sensation of movement was a very slight vibration he would never have noticed had he not been expecting it.

Diaspar must be many miles away by now, and above him would be the desert with its shifting sand dunes. Perhaps at this very moment he was racing beneath the broken hills he had watched as a child from the Tower of Loranne.

His thoughts came back to Lys, as they had done continually for the past few days. He wondered if it still existed, and once again assured himself that not otherwise would the machine be carrying him there. What sort of city would it be? Somehow the strongest effort of his imagination could only picture another and smaller version of Diaspar.

Suddenly there was a distinct change in the vibration of the machine. It was slowing down—there was no question of that. The time must have passed more quickly than he had thought: somewhat surprised, Alvin glanced at the indicator.

LYS

23 MINUTES

Feeling very puzzled, and a little worried, he pressed his face against the side of the machine. His speed was still blurring the walls of the tunnel into a featureless grey, yet now from time to time he could catch a glimpse of markings that disappeared almost as quickly as they came. And at each appearance, they seemed to remain in his field of vision for a little longer.

Then, without any warning, the walls of the tunnel were snatched away on either side. The machine was passing, still at a very great speed, through an enormous empty space, far larger even than the chamber of the moving ways.

Peering in wonder through the transparent walls, Alvin could glimpse beneath him an intricate network of guiding rods, rods that crossed and crisscrossed to disappear into a maze of tunnels on either side. Overhead, a long row of artificial suns flooded the chamber with light, and silhouetted against the glare he could just make out the frameworks of great carrying machines. The light was so brilliant that it pained the eyes, and Alvin knew that this place had not been intended for Man. What it was intended for became clear a moment later, when his vehicle flashed past row after row of cylinders, lying motionless above their guide-rails. They were larger than the machine in which he was travelling, and Alvin realized that they must be freight transporters. Around them were grouped incomprehensible machines, all silent and stilled.

Almost as quickly as it had appeared, the vast and lonely chamber vanished behind him. Its passing left a feeling of awe in Alvin's mind: for the first time he really understood the meaning of that great, darkened map below Diaspar. The world was more full of wonder than he had ever dreamed.

Alvin glanced again at the indicator. It had not changed: he had taken less than a minute to flash through the great cavern. The machine was accelerating again, although there was still no sense of motion. But on either side the tunnel walls were flowing past at a speed he could not even guess.

It seemed an age before that indefinable change of vibration occurred again. Now the indicator was reading:—

LYS

1 MINUTE

and that minute was the longest Alvin had ever known. More and more slowly moved the machine: this was no mere slackening of its speed. It was coming to rest at last.

Smoothly and silently the long cylinder slid out of the
tunnel into a cavern that might have been the twin of the
one beneath Diaspar. For a moment Alvin was too ex-
cited to see anything clearly. His thoughts were jumbled
and he could not even control the door, which opened
and closed several times before he pulled himself together. As he jumped out of the machine, he caught a
last glimpse of the indicator. Its wording had changed
and there was something about its message that was
very reassuring:—

DIASPAR

35 MINUTES

It had been as simple as that. No one could have guessed that he had made a journey as fateful as any in the history of Man.

As he began to search for a way out of the chamber, Alvin found the first sign that he was in a civilization very different from the one he had left. The way to the surface clearly lay through a low, wide tunnel at one end of the cavern—and leading up through the tunnel was a flight of steps. Such a thing was almost unknown in Diaspar. The machines disliked stairways, and the architects of the city had built ramps or sloping corridors wherever there was a change of level. Was it possible that there were no machines in Lys? The idea was so fantastic that Alvin dismissed it at once.

The stairway was very short, and ended against doors that opened at his approach. As they closed silently behind him, Alvin found himself in a large cubical room which appeared to have no other exit. He stood for a moment, a little puzzled, and then began to examine the opposite wall. As he did so, the doors through which he had entered opened once more. Feeling somewhat annoyed, Alvin left the room again—to find himself looking along a vaulted corridor rising slowly to an archway that framed a semicircle of sky. He realized that he must have risen many hundreds of feet, but there had been no sensation of movement. Then he hurried forward up the slope to the sunlit opening.

He was standing at the brow of a low hill, and for an instant it seemed as if he were once again in the central park of Diaspar. Yet if this was indeed a park, it was too enormous for his mind to grasp. The city he had expected to see was nowhere visible. As far as the eye could reach there was nothing but forest and grass-covered plains.

Then Alvin lifted his eyes to the horizon, and there above the trees, sweeping from right to left in a great arc that encircled the world, was a line of stone which would have dwarfed the mightiest giants of Diaspar. It was so far away that its details were blurred by sheer distance, but there was something about its outlines that Alvin found puzzling. Then his eyes became at last accustomed to the scale of that colossal landscape, and he knew that those faroff walls had not been built by Man.

Time had not conquered everything: Earth still possessed mountains of which she could be proud.

For a long time Alvin stood at the mouth of the tunnel, growing slowly accustomed to the strange world in which he had found himself. Search as he might, nowhere could he see any trace of human life. Yet the road that led down the hillside seemed well kept: he could do no more than accept its guidance.

At the foot of the hill, the road disappeared between great trees that almost hid the sun. As Alvin walked into their shadow, a strange medley of scents and sounds greeted him. The rustle of the wind among the leaves he had known before, but underlying that were a thousand vague noises that conveyed nothing to his mind. Unknown odors assailed him, smells that had been lost even to the memory of his race. The warmth, the profusion of scent and color, and the unseen presences of a million living things, smote him with almost physical violence.

He came upon the lake without any warning. The trees to the right suddenly ended, and before him was a great expanse of water, dotted with tiny islands. Never in his life had Alvin seen such quantities of the precious liquid:

he walked to the edge of the lake and let the warm water trickle through his fingers.

The great silver fish that suddenly forced its way through the underwater reeds was the first non-human creature he had ever seen. As it hung in nothingness, its fins a faint blur of motion, Alvin wondered why its shape was so startlingly familiar. Then he remembered the records that Jeserac had shown him as a child, and knew where he had seen those graceful lines before. Logic told him that the resemblance could only be accidental—but logic was wrong.

All through the ages, artists had been inspired by the urgent beauty of the great ships driving from world to world. Once there had been craftsmen who had worked, not with crumbling metal or decaying stone, but with the most imperishable of all materials—flesh and blood and bone. Though they and all their race had been utterly forgotten, one of their dreams had survived the ruins of cities and the wreck of continents.

At last Alvin broke the lake's enchantment and continued along the winding road. The forest closed around him once more, but only for a little while. Presently the road ended, in a great clearing perhaps half a mile wide and twice as long. Now Alvin understood why he had seen no trace of man before.

The clearing was full of low, two-storied buildings, colored in soft shades that rested the eye even in the full glare of the sun. They were of clean, straightforward design, but several were built in a complex architectural style involving the use of fluted columns and gracefully fretted stone. In these buildings, which seemed of great age, the immeasurably ancient device of the pointed arch was used.

As he walked slowly towards the village, Alvin was still struggling to grasp his new surroundings. Nothing was familiar: even the air had changed. And the tall, golden-

haired people coming and going among the buildings
were very different from the languid citizens of Diaspar.

Alvin had almost reached the village when he saw a
group of men coming purposefully towards him. He felt a
sudden, heady excitement and the blood pounded in his
veins. For an instant there flashed through his mind the
memory of all Man's fateful meetings with other races.
Then he came to a halt, a few feet away from the others.

They seemed surprised to see him, yet not as surprised
as he had expected. Very quickly he understood why.
The leader of the party extended his hand in the ancient
gesture of friendship.

"We thought it best to meet you here," he said. "Our
home is very different from Diaspar, and the walk from
the terminus gives visitors a chance to become—acclima-
tized."

Alvin accepted the outstretched hand, but for a moment was too astonished to reply.

"You knew I was coming?" he gasped at length.

"We always know when the carriers start to move. But
we did not expect anyone so young. How did you discover the way?"

"I think we'd better restrain our curiosity, Gerane.
Seranis is waiting."

The name "Seranis" was preceded by a word unfamiliar
to Alvin. It somehow conveyed an impression of affection,
tempered with respect.

Gerane agreed with the speaker and the party began to
move into the village. As they walked, Alvin studied the
faces around him. They appeared kindly and intelligent:
there were none of the signs of boredom, mental strife,
and faded brilliance he might have found in a similar
group in his own city. To his broadening mind, it seemed
that they possessed all that his own people had lost. When
they smiled, which was often, they revealed lines of

ivory teeth—the pearls that Man had lost and won and lost again in the long story of evolution.

The people of the village watched with frank curiosity as Alvin followed his guides. He was amazed to see not a few children, who stared at him in grave surprise. No other single fact brought home to him so vividly his remoteness from the world he knew. Diaspar had paid, and paid in full, the price of immortality.

The party halted before the largest building Alvin had yet seen. It stood in the center of the village and from a flagpole on its small circular tower a green pennant floated along the breeze.

All but Gerane dropped behind as he entered the building. Inside it was quiet and cool: sunlight filtering through the translucent walls lit up everything with a soft, restful glow. The floor was smooth and resilient, inlaid with fine mosaics. On the walls, an artist of great ability and power had depicted a set of forest scenes. Mingled with these paintings were other murals which conveyed nothing to Alvin's mind, yet were attractive and pleasant to look upon. Let into the wall was something he had hardly expected to see—a visiphone receiver, beautifully made, its idle screen filled with a maze of shifting colors.

They walked together up a short circular stairway that led them out on the flat roof of the building. From this point, the entire village was visible, and Alvin could see that it consisted of about a hundred buildings. In the distance the trees opened out into wide meadows: he could see animals in some of the fields but his knowledge of biology was too slight for him to guess at their nature.

In the shadow of the tower, two people were sitting together at a desk, watching him intently. As they rose to greet him, Alvin saw that one was a stately, very handsome woman whose golden hair was shot through with wisps of grey. This, he knew, must be Seranis. Looking into her eyes, he could sense that wisdom and depth of

experience he felt when he was with Rorden and, more
rarely, with Jeserac.

The other was a boy a little older than himself in appearance, and Alvin needed no second glance to tell
that Seranis must be his mother. The clear-cut features
were the same, though the eyes held only friendliness
and not that almost frightening wisdom. The hair too was
different—black instead of gold—but no one could have
mistaken the relationship between them.

Feeling a little overawed, Alvin turned to his guide for
support—but Gerane had already vanished. Then Seranis
smiled, and his nervousness left him.

"Welcome to Lys," she said. "I am Seranis, and this is
my son Theon, who will one day take my place. You are
the youngest who has ever come to us from Diaspar:
tell me how you found the way."

Haltingly at first, and then with increasing confidence,
Alvin began his story. Theon followed his words eagerly,
for Diaspar must have been as strange to him as Lys
had been to Alvin. But Seranis, Alvin could see, knew all
that he was telling her, and once or twice she asked
questions which showed that in some things at least her
knowledge went beyond his own. When he had finished
there was silence for a while. Then Seranis looked at him
and said quietly:

"Why did you come to Lys?"

"I wanted to explore the world," he replied. "Everyone told me that there was only desert beyond the city,
but I wanted to make sure for myself."

The eyes of Seranis were full of sympathy and even
sadness when she spoke again:

"And was that the only reason?"

Alvin hesitated. When he answered, it was not the explorer who spoke, but the boy not long removed from
childhood.

"No," he said slowly, "it wasn't the only reason, though I did not know until now. I was lonely."

"Lonely? In Diaspar?"

"Yes," said Alvin. "I am the only child to be born there for seven thousand years."

Those wonderful eyes were still upon him, and, looking into their depths, Alvin had the sudden conviction that Seranis could read his mind. Even as the thought came, he saw an expression of amused surprise pass across her face—and knew that his guess had been correct. Once both men and machines had possessed this power, and the unchanging machines could still read their masters' orders. But in Diaspar, Man himself had lost the gift he had given to his slaves.

Rather quickly, Seranis broke into his thoughts.

"If you are looking for life," she said, "your search has ended. Apart from Diaspar, there is only desert beyond our mountains."

It was strange that Alvin, who had questioned accepted beliefs so often before, did not doubt the words of Seranis. His only reaction was one of sadness that all his teaching had been so nearly true.

"Tell me something about Lys," he asked. "Why have you been cut off from Diaspar for so long, when you know all about us?"

Seranis smiled at his question.

"It's not easy to answer that in a few words, but I'll do my best.

"Because you have lived in Diaspar all your life, you have come to think of Man as a city dweller. That isn't true, Alvin. Since the machines gave us freedom, there has always been a rivalry between two different types of civilization. In the Dawn Ages there were thousands of cities, but a large part of mankind lived in communities like this village of ours.

"We have no records of the founding of Lys, but we

know that our remote ancestors disliked city life intensely and would have nothing to do with it. In spite of swift and universal transport, they kept themselves largely apart from the rest of the world and developed an independent culture which was one of the highest the race had ever known.

"Through the ages, as we advanced along our different roads, the gulf between Lys and the cities widened. It was bridged only in times of great crisis: we know that when the Moon was falling, its destruction was planned and carried out by the scientists of Lys. So too was the defense of Earth against the Invaders, whom we held at the Battle of Shalmirane.

"That great ordeal exhausted mankind: one by one the cities died and the desert rolled over them. As the population fell, humanity began the migration which was to make Diaspar the last and greatest of all cities.

"Most of these changes passed us by, but we had our own battle to fight—the battle against the desert. The natural barrier of the mountains was not enough, and many thousands of years passed before we had made our land secure. Far beneath Lys are machines which will give us water as long as the world remains, for the old oceans are still there, miles down in the Earth's crust.

"That, very briefly, is our history. You will see that even in the Dawn Ages we had little to do with the cities, though their people often came into our land. We never hindered them, for many of our greatest men came from Outside, but when the cities were dying we did not wish to be involved in their downfall. With the ending of air transport, there was only one way into Lys—the carrier system from Diaspar. Four hundred million years ago that was closed by mutual agreement. But we have remembered Diaspar, and I do not know why you have forgotten Lys."

Seranis smiled, a little wryly.

"Diaspar has surprised us. We expected it to go the way of all other cities, but instead it has achieved a stable culture that may last as long as Earth. It is not a culture we admire, yet we are glad that those who wish to escape have been able to do so. More than you might think have made the journey, and they have almost all been outstanding men."

Alvin wondered how Seranis could be so sure of her facts, and he did not approve of her attitude towards Diaspar. He had hardly "escaped"—yet, after all, the word was not altogether inaccurate.

Somewhere a great bell vibrated with a throbbing boom that ebbed and died in the still air. Six times it struck, and as the last note faded into silence Alvin realized that the sun was low on the horizon and the eastern sky already held a hint of night.

"I must return to Diaspar," he said. "Rorden is expecting me."

Seranis looked at him thoughtfully for a moment. Then she rose to her feet and walked towards the stairway.

"Please wait a little while," she said. "I have some business to settle, and Theon, I know, has many questions to ask you."

Then she was gone, and for the next few minutes Theon's barrage of questions drove any other thoughts from his mind. Theon had heard of Diaspar, and had seen records of the cities as they were at the height of their glory, but he could not imagine how their inhabitants had passed their lives. Alvin was amused at many of his questions—until he realized that his own ignorance of Lys was even greater.

Seranis was gone for many minutes, but her expression revealed nothing when she returned.

"We have been talking about you," she said—not explaining who "we" might be: "If you return to Diaspar, the whole city will know about us. Whatever promises you make, the secret could not be kept."

A feeling of slight panic began to creep over Alvin. Seranis must have known his thoughts, for her next words were more reassuring.

"We don't wish to keep you here against your wishes, but if you return to Diaspar we will have to erase all memories of Lys from your mind." She hesitated for a moment. "This has never arisen before: all your predecessors came here to stay."

Alvin was thinking deeply.

"Why should it matter," he said, "if Diaspar does learn

about you again? Surely it would be a good thing for both our peoples?"

Seranis looked displeased.

"We don't think so," she said. "If the gates were opened, our land would be flooded with sensation-seekers and the idly curious. As things are now, only the best of your people have ever reached us."

Alvin felt himself becoming steadily more annoyed, but he realized that Seranis' attitude was quite unconscious.

"That isn't true," he said flatly. "Very few of us would ever leave Diaspar. If you let me return, it would make no difference to Lys."

"The decision is not in my hands," replied Seranis, "but I will put it to the Council when it meets three days from now. Until then, you can remain as my guest, and Theon will show you our country."

"I would like to do that," said Alvin, "but Rorden will be waiting for me. He knows where I am, and if I don't come back at once anything may happen."

Seranis smiled slightly.

"We have given that a good deal of thought," she admitted. "There are men working on the problem now—we will see if they have been successful."

Alvin was annoyed at having overlooked something so obvious. He knew that the engineers of the past had built for eternity—his journey to Lys had been proof of that. Yet it gave him a shock when the chromatic mist on the visiphone screen drifted aside to show the familiar outlines of Rorden's room.

The Keeper of the Records looked up from his desk. His eyes lit when he saw Alvin.

"I never expected you to be early," he said—though there was relief behind the jesting words. "Shall I come to meet you?"

While Alvin hesitated, Seranis stepped forward, and

Rorden saw her for the first time. His eyes widened and he leaned forward as if to obtain a better view. The movement was as useless as it was automatic: Man had not lost it even though he had used the visiphone for a thousand million years.

Seranis laid her hands on Alvin's shoulders and began to speak. When she had finished Rorden was silent for a while.

"I'll do my best," he said at length. "As I understand it, the choice lies between sending Alvin back to us under some form of hypnosis—or returning him with no restrictions at all. But I think I can promise that even if it learns of your existence, Diaspar will continue to ignore you."

"We won't overlook that possibility," Seranis replied with just a trace of pique. Rorden detected it instantly.

"And what of myself?" he asked with a smile. "I know as much as Alvin now."

"Alvin is a boy," replied Seranis quickly, "but you hold an office as ancient as Diaspar. This is not the first time Lys has spoken to the Keeper of the Records, and he has never betrayed our secret yet."

Rorden made no comment: he merely said: "How long do you wish to keep Alvin?"

"At the most, five days. The Council meets three days from now."

"Very well: for the next five days, then, Alvin is extremely busy on some historical research with me. This won't be the first time it's happened—but we'll have to be out if Jeserac calls."

Alvin laughed.

"Poor Jeserac! I seem to spend half my life hiding things from him."

"You've been much less successful than you think," replied Rorden, somewhat disconcertingly. "However I don't expect any trouble. But don't be longer than the five days!"

When the picture had faded, Rorden sat for a while staring at the darkened screen. He had always suspected that the world communication network might still be in existence, but the keys to its operation had been lost and the billions of circuits could never be traced by Man. It was strange to reflect that even now visiphones might be called vainly in the lost cities. Perhaps the time would come when his own receiver would do the same, and there would be no Keeper of the Records to answer the unknown caller. . . .

He began to feel afraid. The immensity of what had happened was slowly dawning upon him. Until now, Rorden had given little thought to the consequences of his actions. His own historical interests, and his affection for Alvin, had been sufficient motive for what he had done. Though he had humored and encouraged Alvin, he had never believed that anything like this could possibly happen.

Despite the centuries between them, the boy's will had always been more powerful than his own. It was too late to do anything about it now: Rorden felt that events were sweeping him along towards a climax utterly beyond his control.

"Is all this really necessary," said Alvin, "if we are only going to be away for two or three days? After all, we have a synthesizer with us."

"Probably not," answered Theon, throwing the last food containers into the little ground-car. "It may seem an odd custom, but we've never synthesized some of our finest foods—we like to watch them grow. Also, we may meet other parties and it's polite to exchange food with them. Nearly every district has some special product, and Airlee is famous for its peaches. That's why I've put so many aboard—not because I think that even you can eat them all."

Alvin threw his half-eaten peach at Theon, who dodged quickly aside. There came a flicker of iridescence and a faint whirring of invisible wings as Krif descended upon the fruit and began to sip its juices.

Alvin was still not quite used to Krif. It was hard for him to realize that the great insect, though it would come when called and would—sometimes—obey simple orders, was almost wholly mindless. Life, to Alvin, had always been synonymous with intelligence—sometimes intelligence far higher than Man's.

When Krif was resting, his six gauzy wings lay folded along his body, which glittered through them like a jewelled scepter. He was at once the highest and the most beautiful form of insect life the world had ever known—the latest and perhaps the last of all the creatures Man had chosen for his companionship.

Lys was full of such surprises, as Alvin was continually learning. Its inconspicuous but efficient transport system had been equally unexpected. The ground-car apparently worked on the same principle as the machine that had brought him from Diaspar, for it floated in the air a few inches above the turf. Although there was no sign of any guide-rail, Theon told him that the cars could only run on predetermined tracks. All the centers of population were thus linked together, but the remoter parts of the country could only be reached on foot. This state of affairs seemed altogether extraordinary to Alvin, but Theon appeared to think it was an excellent idea.

Apparently Theon had been planning this expedition for a considerable time. Natural history was his chief passion—Krif was only the most spectacular of his many pets—and he hoped to find new types of insect life in the uninhabited southern parts of Lys.

The project had filled Alvin with enthusiasm when he heard of it. He looked forward to seeing more of this won-

derful country, and although Theon's interests lay in a
different field of knowledge from his own, he felt a kin-
ship for his new companion which not even Rorden had
ever awakened.

Theon intended to travel south as far as the machine
could go—little more than an hour's journey from Airlee—
and the rest of the way they would have to go on foot.
Not realizing the full implications of this, Alvin had no
objections.

To Alvin, the journey across Lys had a dreamlike unreality. Silent as a ghost, the machine slid across rolling
plains and wound its way through forests, never deviating
from its invisible track. It travelled perhaps a dozen times
as fast as a man could comfortably walk. No one in
Lys was ever in a greater hurry than that.

Many times they passed through villages, some larger
than Airlee but most built along very similar lines. Alvin
was interested to notice subtle but significant differences
in clothing and even physical appearance as they moved
from one community to the next. The civilization of Lys
was composed of hundreds of distinct cultures, each con-
tributing some special talent towards the whole.

Once or twice Theon stopped to speak to friends, but
the pauses were brief and it was still morning when the
little machine came to rest among the foothills of a heavily wooded mountain. It was not a very large mountain,
but Alvin thought it the most tremendous thing he had
ever seen.

"This is where we start to walk," said Theon cheerfully,
throwing equipment out of the car. "We can't ride any
farther."

As he fumbled with the straps that were to convert him
into a beast of burden, Alvin looked doubtfully at the
great mass of rock before them.

"It's a long way round, isn't it?" he queried.

"We aren't going round," replied Theon. "I want to get to the top before nightfall."

Alvin said nothing. He had been rather afraid of this.

"From here," said Theon, raising his voice to make it heard above the thunder of the waterfall, "you can see the whole of Lys."

Alvin could well believe him. To the north lay mile upon mile of forest, broken here and there by clearings and fields and the wandering threads of a hundred rivers. Hidden somewhere in that vast panorama was the village of Airlee. Alvin fancied that he could catch a glimpse of the great lake, but decided that his eyes had tricked him. Still farther north, trees and clearings alike were lost in a mottled carpet of green, rucked here and there by lines of hills. And beyond that, at the very edge of vision, the mountains that hemmed Lys from the desert lay like a bank of distant clouds.

East and west the view was little different, but to the south the mountains seemed only a few miles away. Alvin could see them very clearly, and he realized that they were far higher than the little peak on which he was standing.

But more wonderful even than these was the waterfall. From the sheer face of the mountain a mighty ribbon of water leaped far out over the valley, curving down through space towards the rocks a thousand feet below. There it was lost in a shimmering mist of spray, while up from the depths rose a ceaseless, drumming thunder that reverberated in hollow echoes from the mountain walls. And quivering in the air above the base of the fall was the last rainbow left on Earth.

For long minutes the two boys lay on the edge of the cliff, gazing at this last Niagara and the unknown land beyond. It was very different from the country they had left, for in some indefinable way it seemed deserted and empty. Man had not lived here for many, many years.

Theon answered his friend's unspoken question.

"Once the whole of Lys was inhabited," he said, "but that was a very long time ago. Only the animals live here now."

Indeed, there was nowhere any sign of human life— none of the clearings or well-disciplined rivers that spoke of Man's presence. Only in one spot was there any indication that he had ever lived here, for many miles away a solitary white ruin jutted above the forest roof like a broken fang. Elsewhere, the jungle had returned to its own.

It was night when Alvin awoke, the utter night of mountain country, terrifying in its intensity. Something had disturbed him, some whisper of sound that had crept into his mind above the dull thunder of the falls. He sat up in the darkness, straining his eyes across the hidden land, while with indrawn breath he listened to the drumming roar of the falls and the faint but unending rustle of life in the trees around him.

Nothing was visible. The starlight was too dim to reveal the miles of country that lay hundreds of feet below: only a jagged line of darker night eclipsing the stars told of the mountains on the southern horizon. In the darkness beside him Alvin heard his friend roll over and sit up.

"What is it?" came a whispered voice.

"I thought I heard a noise."

"What sort of noise?"

"I don't know. Perhaps I was only dreaming."

There was silence while two pairs of eyes peered out into the mystery of night. Then, suddenly, Theon caught his friend's arm.

"Look!" he whispered.

Far to the south glowed a solitary point of light, too low in the heavens to be a star. It was a brilliant white, tinged with violet, and as the boys watched it began to climb the spectrum of intensity, until the eye could no longer bear to look upon it. Then it exploded—and it seemed as if lightning had struck below the rim of the world. For an instant the mountains, and the great land they guarded, were etched with fire against the darkness of the night. Ages later came the echo of a mighty explosion, and in the forest below a sudden wind stirred among the trees. It died away swiftly, and one by one the routed stars crept back into the sky.

For the first time in his life, Alvin knew that fear of the unknown that had been the curse of ancient Man. It was a feeling so strange that for a while he could not even give it a name. In the moment of recognition it vanished and he became himself again.

What is it?" he whispered.

There was a pause so long that he repeated the question.

"I'm trying to remember," said Theon, and was silent for a while. A little later he spoke again.

"That must be Shalmirane," he said simply.

"Shalmirane! Does it still exist?"

"I'd almost forgotten," replied Theon, "but it's coming back now. Mother once told me that the fortress lies in those mountains. Of course, it's been in ruins for ages, but someone is still supposed to live there."

Shalmirane! To these children of two races, so widely differing in culture and history, this was indeed a name of magic. In all the long story of Earth there had been no greater epic than the defense of Shalmirane against an invader who had conquered all the Universe.

Presently Theon's voice came again out of the darkness.

"The people of the south could tell us more. We will ask them on our way back."

Alvin scarcely heard him: he was deep in his own thoughts, remembering stories that Rorden had told him long ago. The Battle of Shalmirane lay at the dawn of recorded history: it marked the end of the legendary ages of Man's conquests, and the beginning of his long decline. In Shalmirane, if anywhere on Earth, lay the answers to the problems that had tormented him for so many years. But the southern mountains were very far away.

Theon must have shared something of his mother's powers, for he said quietly:

"If we started at dawn, we could reach the fortress by nightfall. I've never been there, but I think I could find the way."

Alvin thought it over. He was tired, his feet were sore, and the muscles of his thighs were aching with the unaccustomed effort. It was very tempting to leave it until another time. Yet there might be no other time, and there was even the possibility that the actinic explosion had been a signal for help.

Beneath the dim light of the failing stars, Alvin wrestled with his thoughts and presently made his decision. Nothing had changed: the mountains resumed their watch over the sleeping land. But a turning-point in history had come and gone, and the human race was moving towards a strange new future.

The sun had just lifted above the eastern wall of Lys when they reached the outskirts of the forest. Here, Nature had returned to her own. Even Theon seemed lost among the gigantic trees that blocked the sunlight and cast pools of shadow on the jungle floor. Fortunately the river from the fall flowed south in a line too straight to be altogether natural, and by keeping to its edge they could avoid the denser undergrowth. A good deal of Theon's time was spent in controlling Krif, who disappeared occasionally into the jungle or went skimming wildly across the water. Even Alvin, to whom everything was still so new, could feel that the forest had a fascination not possessed by the smaller, more cultivated woods of northern Lys. Few trees were alike: most of them were in various stages of devolution and some had reverted through the ages almost to their original, natural forms. Many were obviously not of Earth at all—perhaps not even of the

Solar System. Watching like sentinels over the lesser trees were giant sequoias, three and four hundred feet high. They had once been called the oldest things on Earth: they were still a little older than Man.

The river was widening now: ever and again it opened into small lakes, upon which tiny islands lay at anchor. There were insects here, brilliantly colored creatures swinging aimlessly to and fro over the surface of the water. Once, despite Theon's shouts, Krif darted away to join his distant cousins. He disappeared instantly in a cloud of glittering wings, and the sound of angry buzzing floated towards them. A moment later the cloud erupted and Krif came back across the water, almost too quickly for the eye to follow. Thereafter he kept very close to Theon and did not stray again.

Towards evening they caught occasional glimpses of the mountains ahead. The river that had been so faithful a guide was flowing sluggishly now, as if it too were nearing the end of its journey. But it was clear that they could not reach the mountains by nightfall: well before sunset the forest had become so dark that further progress was impossible. The great trees lay in pools of shadow, and a cold wind was sweeping through the leaves. Alvin and Theon settled down for the night beside a giant redwood whose topmost branches were still ablaze with sunlight.

When at last the hidden sun went down, the light still lingered on the dancing waters. The two boys lay in the gathering gloom, watching the river and thinking of all that they had seen. As Alvin fell asleep, he found himself wondering who last had come this way, and how long since.

The sun was high when they left the forest and stood at last before the mountain walls of Lys. Ahead of them the ground rose steeply to the sky in waves of barren rock. Here the river came to an end as spectacular as its beginning, for the ground opened in its path and it sank roaring from sight.

For a moment Theon stood looking at the whirlpool and the broken land beyond. Then he pointed to a gap in the hills.

"Shalmirane lies in that direction," he said confidently. Alvin looked at him in surprise.

"You told me you'd never been here before!"

"I haven't."

"Then how do you know the way?"

Theon looked puzzled.

"I don't know—I've never thought about it before. It must be a kind of instinct, for wherever we go in Lys we always know our way about."

Alvin found this very difficult to believe, and followed Theon with considerable skepticism. They were soon through the gap in the hills, and ahead of them now was a curious plateau with gently sloping sides. After a moment's hesitation, Theon started to climb. Alvin followed, full of doubts, and as he climbed he began to compose a little speech. If the journey proved in vain, Theon would know exactly what he thought of his unerring instinct.

As they approached the summit, the nature of the ground altered abruptly. The lower slopes had consisted of porous, volcanic stone, piled here and there in great mounds of slag. Now the surface turned suddenly to hard sheets of glass, smooth and treacherous, as if the rock had once run in molten rivers down the mountain. The rim of the plateau was almost at their feet. Theon reached it first, and a few seconds later Alvin overtook him and stood speechless at his side. For they stood on the edge, not of the plateau they had expected, but of a giant bowl half a mile deep and three miles in diameter. Ahead of them the ground plunged steeply downwards, slowly levelling out at the bottom of the valley and rising again, more and more steeply, to the opposite rim. And although it now lay in the full glare of the sun, the whole of that great depression was ebon black. What material formed the crater the boys could not even guess, but it was black as the rock of a world that had never known a sun. Nor was that all, for lying beneath their feet and ringing the entire crater was a seamless band of metal, some hundred feet wide, tarnished by immeasurable age but still showing no slightest trace of corrosion.

As their eyes grew accustomed to the unearthly scene, Alvin and Theon realized that the blackness of the bowl was not as absolute as they had thought. Here and there, so fugitive that they could only see them indirectly, tiny explosions of light were flickering in the ebon walls. They came at random, vanishing as soon as they were born, like the reflections of stars on a broken sea.

"It's wonderful!" gasped Alvin. "But what is it?"

"It looks like a reflector of some kind."

"I can't imagine that black stuff reflecting anything."

"It's only black to our eyes, remember. We don't know what radiations they used."

"But surely there's more than this! Where *is* the fortress?"

Theon pointed to the level floor of the crater, where lay what Alvin had taken to be a pile of jumbled stones. As he looked again, he could make out an almost obliterated plan behind the grouping of the great blocks. Yes, there lay the ruins of once mighty buildings, overthrown by time.

For the first few hundred yards the walls were too smooth and steep for the boys to stand upright, but after a little while they reached the gentler slopes and could walk without difficulty. Near the bottom of the crater the smooth ebony of its surface ended in a thin layer of soil, which the winds of Lys must have brought here through the ages.

A quarter of a mile away, titanic blocks of stone were

piled one upon the other, like the discarded toys of an infant giant. Here, a section of a massive wall was still recognizable: there, two carven obelisks marked what had once been a mighty entrance. Everywhere grew mosses and creeping plants, and tiny stunted trees. Even the wind was hushed.

So Alvin and Theon came to the ruins of Shalmirane. Against those walls, if legend spoke the truth, forces that could shatter a world to dust had flamed and thundered and been utterly defeated. Once these peaceful skies had blazed with fires torn from the hearts of suns, and the mountains of Lys must have quailed like living things beneath the fury of their masters.

No one had ever captured Shalmirane. But now the fortress, the impregnable fortress, had fallen at last—captured and destroyed by the patient tendrils of the ivy and the generations of blindly burrowing worms.

Overawed by its majesty, the two boys walked in silence towards the colossal wreck. They passed into the shadow of a broken wall, and entered a canyon where the mountains of stone had split asunder.

Before them lay a great amphitheater, crossed and crisscrossed with long mounds of rubble that must mark the graves of buried machines. Once the whole of this tremendous space had been vaulted, but the roof had long since collapsed. Yet life must still exist somewhere among the desolation, and Alvin realized that even this ruin might be no more than superficial. The greater part of the fortress would be far underground, beyond the reach of Time.

"We'll have to turn back by noon," said Theon, "so we mustn't stay too long. It would be quicker if we separated. I'll take the eastern half and you can explore this side. Shout if you find anything interesting—but don't get too far away."

So they separated, and Alvin began to climb over the

rubble, skirting the larger mounds of stone. Near the center of the arena he came suddenly upon a small circular clearing, thirty or forty feet in diameter. It had been covered with weeds, but they were now blackened and charred by tremendous heat, so that they crumbled to ashes at his approach. At the center of the clearing stood a tripod supporting a polished metal bowl, not unlike a model of Shalmirane itself. It was capable of movement in altitude and azimuth, and a spiral of some transparent substance was supported at its center. Beneath the reflector was welded a black box from which a thin cable wandered away across the ground.

It was clear to Alvin that this machine must be the source of the light, and he began to trace the cable. It was not too easy to follow the slender wire, which had a habit of diving into crevasses and reappearing at unexpected places. Finally he lost it altogether and shouted to Theon to come and help him.

He was crawling under an overhanging rock when a shadow suddenly blotted out the light. Thinking it was his friend, Alvin emerged from the cave and turned to speak. But the words died abruptly on his lips.

Hanging in the air before him was a great dark eye surrounded by a satellite system of smaller eyes. That, at least, was Alvin's first impression: then he realized that he was looking at a complex machine—and it was looking at him.

Alvin broke the painful silence. All his life he had given orders to machines, and although he had never seen anything quite like this creature, he decided that it was probably intelligent.

"Reverse," he ordered experimentally.

Nothing happened.

"Go. Come. Rise. Fall. Advance."

None of the conventional control thought produced

any effect. The machine remained contemptuously inactive.

Alvin took a step forward, and the eyes retreated in some haste. Unfortunately their angle of vision seemed somewhat limited, for the machine came to a sudden halt against Theon, who for the last minute had been an interested spectator. With a perfectly human ejaculation, the whole apparatus shot twenty feet into the air, revealing a set of tentacles and jointed limbs clustering round a stubby cylindrical body.

"Come down—we won't hurt you!" called Theon, rubbing a bruise on his chest.

Something spoke: not the passionless, crystal-clear voice of a machine, but the quavering speech of a very old and very tired man.

"Who are you? What are you doing in Shalmirane?"

"My name is Theon, and this is my friend, Alvin of Loronei. We're exploring Southern Lys."

There was a brief pause. When the machine spoke again its voice held an unmistakable note of petulance and annoyance.

"Why can't you leave me in peace? You know how often I've asked to be left alone!"

Theon, usually good-natured, bristled visibly.

"We're from Airlee, and we don't know anything about Shalmirane."

"Besides," Alvin added reproachfully, "we saw your light and thought you might be signalling for help."

It was strange to hear so human a sigh from the coldly impersonal machine.

"A million times I must have signalled now, and all I have ever done is to draw the inquisitive from Lys. But I see you meant no harm. Follow me."

The machine floated slowly away over the broken stones, coming to rest before a dark opening in the ruined wall of the amphitheater. In the shadow of the cave

something moved, and a human figure stepped into the
sunlight. He was the first physically old man Alvin had
ever seen. His head was completely bald, but a thick
growth of pure white hair covered all the lower part of
his face. A cloak of woven glass was thrown carelessly
over his shoulders, and on either side of him floated two
more of the strange, many-eyed machines.

There was a brief silence while each side regarded the other. Then the old man spoke—and the three machines echoed his voice for a moment until something switched them off.

"So you are from the North, and your people have already forgotten Shalmirane."

"Oh, no!" said Theon quickly. "We've not forgotten. But we weren't sure that anyone still lived here, and we certainly didn't know that you wished to be left alone."

The old man did not reply. Moving with a slowness that was painful to watch, he hobbled through the doorway and disappeared, the three machines floating silently after him. Alvin and Theon looked at each other in surprise: they did not like to follow, but their dismissal—if dismissal it was—had certainly been brusque. They were starting to argue the matter when one of the machines suddenly reappeared.

"What are you waiting for? Come along!" it ordered. Then it vanished again.

Alvin shrugged his shoulders.

"We appear to be invited. I think our host's a little eccentric, but he seems friendly."

From the opening in the wall a wide spiral stairway led downwards for a score of feet. It ended in a small circular room from which several corridors radiated. However, there was no possibility of confusion, for all the passages save one were blocked with debris.

Alvin and Theon had walked only a few yards when they found themselves in a large and incredibly untidy room cluttered up with a bewildering variety of objects. One end of the chamber was occupied by domestic machines—synthesizers, destructors, cleaning equipment and the like—which one normally expected to be concealed from sight in the walls and floors. Around these were piled cases of thought records and transcribers, forming pyramids that reached almost to the ceiling. The whole room was uncomfortably hot owing to the presence of a dozen perpetual fires scattered about the floor. Attracted by the radiation, Krif flew towards the nearest of the metal spheres, stretched his wings luxuriously before it, and fell instantly asleep.

It was a little while before the boys noticed the old man and his three machines waiting for them in a small open space which reminded Alvin of a clearing in the jungle. There was a certain amount of furniture here—a table and three comfortable couches. One of these was old and shabby, but the others were so conspicuously new that Alvin was certain they had been created in the last few minutes. Even as he watched, the familiar warning glow of the synthesizer field flickered over the table and their host waved silently towards it. They thanked him formally and began to sample the food and drink that had suddenly appeared. Alvin realized that he had grown a little tired of the unvarying output from Theon's portable synthesizer and the change was very welcome.

They ate in silence for a while, stealing a glance now and then at the old man. He seemed sunk in his own thoughts and appeared to have forgotten them completely—but as soon as they had finished he looked up and began to question them. When Alvin explained that he was a native not of Lys but of Diaspar, the old fellow showed no particular surprise. Theon did his best to deal with the queries: for one who disliked visitors, their host seemed very anxious to have news of the outer world.

Alvin quickly decided that his earlier attitude must have been a pose.

Presently he fell silent again. The two boys waited with what patience they could: he had told them nothing of himself or what he was doing in Shalmirane. The light-signal that had drawn them there was still as great a mystery as ever, yet they did not care to ask outright for an explanation. So they sat in an uncomfortable silence, their eyes wandering round that amazing room, finding something new and unexpected at every moment. At last Alvin broke into the old man's reverie.

"We must leave soon," he remarked.

It was not a statement so much as a hint. The wrinkled face turned towards him but the eyes were still very far away. Then the tired, infinitely ancient voice began to speak. It was so quiet and low that at first they could scarcely hear: after a while the old man must have no-ticed their difficulty, for of a sudden the three machines began once more to echo his words.

Much that he told them they could never understand. Sometimes he used words which were unknown to them: at other times he spoke as if repeating sentences or whole speeches that others must have written long ago. But the main outlines of the story were clear, and they took Al-vin's thoughts back to the ages of which he had dreamed since his childhood.

The tale began, like so many others, amid the chaos of the Transition Centuries, when the Invaders had gone but the world was still recovering from its wounds. At that time there appeared in Lys the man who later be-came known as the Master. He was accompanied by three strange machines—the very ones that were watching them now—which acted as his servants and also possessed definite intelligences of their own. His origin was a secret he never disclosed, and eventually it was assumed that he had come from space, somehow penetrating the blockade of the Invaders. Far away among the stars there might still be islands of humanity which the tide of war had not yet engulfed.

The Master and his machines possessed powers which the world had lost, and around him he gathered a group of men to whom he taught much wisdom. His personality must have been a very striking one, and Alvin could understand dimly the magnetism that had drawn so many to him. From the dying cities, men had come to Lys in their thousands, seeking rest and peace of mind after the years of confusion. Here among the forests and mountains, listening to the Master's words, they found that peace at last.

At the close of his long life the Master had asked his friends to carry him out into the open so that he could watch the stars. He had waited, his strength waning, until the culmination of the Seven Suns. As he died the resolution with which he had kept his secret so long seemed to weaken, and he babbled many things of which countless books were to be written in future ages. Again and again he spoke of the "Great Ones" who had now left the world but who would surely one day return, and he charged his followers to remain to greet them when they came. Those were his last rational words. He was never again conscious of his surroundings, but just before the end he uttered one phrase that revealed part at least of his secret and had come down the ages to haunt the minds of all who heard it: *"It is lovely to watch the colored shadows on the planets of eternal light."* Then he died.

So arose the religion of the Great Ones, for a religion it now became. At the Master's death many of his followers broke away, but others remained faithful to his teachings, which they slowly elaborated through the ages. At first they believed that the Great Ones, whoever they were, would soon return to Earth, but that hope faded with the passing centuries. Yet the brotherhood continued, gathering new members from the lands around, and slowly its strength and power increased until it dominated the whole of Southern Lys.

It was very hard for Alvin to follow the old man's narrative. The words were used so strangely that he could not tell what was truth and what legend—if, indeed, the story held any truth at all. He had only a confused picture of generations of fanatical men, waiting for some great event which they did not understand to take place at some unknown future date.

The Great Ones never returned. Slowly the power of the movement failed, and the people of Lys drove it into the mountains until it took refuge in Shalmirane. Even then the watchers did not lose their faith, but swore that however long the wait they would be ready when the Great Ones came. Long ago men had learned one way of defying Time, and the knowledge had survived when so much else had been lost. Leaving only a few of their number to watch over Shalmirane, the rest went into the dreamless sleep of suspended animation.

Their numbers slowly falling as sleepers were awakened to replace those who died, the watchers kept faith with the Master. From his dying words it seemed certain that the Great Ones lived on the planets of the Seven Suns, and in later years attempts were made to send signals into space. Long ago the signalling had become no more than a meaningless ritual, and now the story was nearing its end. In a very little while only the three machines would be left in Shalmirane, watching over the bones of the men who had come here so long ago in a cause that they alone could understand.

The thin voice died away, and Alvin's thoughts returned to the world he knew. More than ever before the extent of his ignorance overwhelmed him. A tiny fragment of the past had been illuminated for a little while, but now the darkness had closed over it again.

The world's history was a mass of such disconnected threads, and none could say which were important and which were trivial. This fantastic tale of the Master and the Great Ones might be no more than another of the countless legends that had somehow survived from the civilizations of the Dawn. Yet the three machines were unlike any that Alvin had ever seen. He could not dismiss the whole story, as he had been tempted to do, as a fable built of self-delusion upon a foundation of madness.

"These machines," he said abruptly, "surely they've been questioned? If they came to Earth with the Master, they must still know his secrets."

The old man smiled wearily.

"*They* know," he said, "but they will never speak. The Master saw to that before he handed over the control. We have tried times without number, but it is useless."

Alvin understood. He thought of the Associator in Diaspar, and the seals that Alaine had set upon its knowledge. Even those seals, he now believed, could be broken in time, and the Master Associator must be infinitely more complex than these little robot slaves. He wondered if Rorden, so skilled in unravelling the secrets of the past, would be able to wrest the machines' hidden knowledge from them. But Rorden was far away and would never leave Diaspar.

Quite suddenly the plan came fully fledged into his mind. Only a very young person could ever have thought of it, and it taxed even Alvin's self-confidence to the utmost. Yet once the decision had been made, he moved with determination and much cunning to his goal.

He pointed towards the three machines.

"Are they identical?" he asked. "I mean, can each one do everything, or are they specialized in any way?"

The old man looked a little puzzled.

"I've never thought about it," he said. "When I need

anything, I ask whichever is most convenient. I don't
think there is any difference between them."

"There can't be a great deal of work for them to do
now," Alvin continued innocently. Theon looked a little
startled, but Alvin carefully avoided his friend's eye. The
old man answered guilelessly.

"No," he replied sadly, "Shalmirane is very different
now."

Alvin paused in sympathy: then, very quickly, he began
to talk. At first the old man did not seem to grasp his
proposal: later, when comprehension came, Alvin gave
him no time to interrupt. He spoke of the great store-
houses of knowledge in Diaspar, and the skill with which
the Keeper of the Records could use them. Although the
Master's machines had withstood all other enquirers, they
might yield their secrets to Rorden's probing. It would be
a tragedy if the chance were missed, for it would never
come again.

Flushed with the heat of his own oratory, Alvin ended
his appeal:

"Lend me one of the machines—you do not need them
all. Order it to obey my controls and I will take it to
Diaspar. I promise to return it whether the experiment
succeeds or not."

Even Theon looked shocked, and an expression of horror came across the old man's face.

"I couldn't do that!" he gasped.

"But why not? Think what we might learn!"

The other shook his head firmly.

"It would be against the Master's wishes."

Alvin was disappointed—disappointed and annoyed.
But he was young, and his opponent was old and tired.
He began again to go through the argument, shifting his
attack and pressing home each advantage. And now for
the first time Theon saw an Alvin he had never suspected
before—a personality, indeed, that was surprising Alvin

himself. The men of the Dawn Ages had never let obstacles bar their way for long, and the will-power and determination that had been their heritage had not yet passed from Earth. Even as a child Alvin had withstood the forces seeking to mould him to the pattern of Diaspar. He was older now, and against him was not the greatest city of the world but only an aged man who sought nothing but rest, and would surely find that soon.

The evening was far advanced when the ground-car slid silently through the last screen of trees and came to rest in the great glade of Airlee. The argument, which had lasted most of the journey, had now died away and peace had been restored. They had never quite come to blows, perhaps because the odds were so unequal. Theon had only Krif to support him, but Alvin could call upon the argus-eyed, many-tentacled machine he still regarded so lovingly.

Theon had not minced his words. He had called his friend a bully and had told Alvin that he should be thoroughly ashamed of himself. But Alvin had only laughed and continued to play with his new toy. He did not know how the transfer had been effected, but he alone could control the robot now, could speak with its voice and see through its eyes. It would obey no one else in all the world.

Seranis was waiting for them in a surprising room which seemed to have no ceiling, though Alvin knew that there was a floor above it. She seemed to be worried and more uncertain than he had ever seen her before, and he remembered the choice that might soon lie before him. Until now he had almost forgotten it. He had believed that, somehow, the Council would resolve the difficulty. Now he realized that its decision might not be to his liking.

The voice of Seranis was troubled when she began to speak, and from her occasional pauses Alvin could tell that she was repeating words already rehearsed.

"Alvin," she began, "there are many things I did not tell you before, but which you must learn now if you are to understand our actions.

"You know one of the reasons for the isolation of our two races. The fear of the Invaders, that dark shadow in the depths of every human mind, turned your people against the world and made them lose themselves in their own dreams. Here in Lys that fear has never been so great, although we bore the burden of the attack. We had a better reason for our actions, and what we did, we did with open eyes.

"Long ago, Alvin, men sought immortality and at last achieved it. They forgot that a world which had banished death must also banish birth. The power to extend his life indefinitely brought contentment to the individual but stagnation to the race. You once told me that you were the only child to be born in Diaspar for seven thousand years—but you have seen how many children we have here in Airlee. Ages ago we sacrificed our immortality, but Diaspar still follows the false dream. That is why our ways parted—*and why they must never meet again.*"

Although the words had been more than half-expected, the blow seemed none the less for its anticipation. Yet Alvin refused to admit the failure of all his plans—half-formed though they were—and only part of his brain was listening to Seranis now. He understood and noted all her words, but the conscious portion of his mind was retracing the road to Diaspar, trying to imagine every obstacle that could be placed in his way.

Seranis was clearly unhappy. Her voice was almost pleading as it spoke, and Alvin knew that she was talking not only to him but to her own son. Theon was watching his mother with a concern which held at last more than a trace of accusation.

"We have no desire to keep you here in Lys against

your will, but you must surely realize what it would mean if our people mixed. Between our culture and yours is a gulf as great as any that ever separated Earth from its ancient colonies. Think of this one fact, Alvin. You and Theon are now of nearly the same age—*but he and I will have been dead for centuries when you are still a boy.*"

The room was very quiet, so quiet that Alvin could hear the strange, plaintive cries of unknown beasts in the fields beyond the village. Presently he said, almost in a whisper:

"What do you want me to do?"

"I have put your case to the Council, as I promised, but the law cannot be altered. You may remain here and become one of us, or you may return to Diaspar. If you do that, we must first reshape the patterns of your mind so that you have no recollection of Lys and never again attempt to reach us."

"And Rorden? He would still know the truth, even if I had forgotten everything."

"We have spoken with Rorden many times since you left. He recognizes the wisdom of our actions."

In that dark moment, it seemed to Alvin that the whole world had turned against him. Though there was much truth in the words of Seranis, he would not recognize it: he saw only the wreck of his still dimly conceived plans, the end of the search for knowledge that had now become the most important thing in his life.

Seranis must have read his thoughts.

"I'll leave you for a while," she said. "But remember— whatever your choice, there can be no turning back."

Theon followed her to the door but Alvin called after him. He looked enquiringly at his mother, who hesitated for a moment and then nodded her head. The door closed silently behind her, and Alvin knew that it would not open again without her consent.

Alvin waited until his racing thoughts were once more under control.

"Theon," he began, "you'll help me, won't you?"

The other nodded but did not speak.

"Then tell me this—how could your people stop me if I tried to run away?"

"That would be easy. If you tried to escape, my mother would take control of your mind. Later, when you became one of us, you would not wish to leave."

"I see. Can you tell if she is watching my mind now?"

Theon looked worried, but his protest answered the question.

"I shouldn't tell you that!"

"But you will, won't you?"

The two boys looked silently at each other for many seconds. Then Theon smiled.

"You can't bully me, you know. Whatever you're planning—and I can't read your mind—as soon as you tried to put it into action Mother would take over. She won't let you out of her sight until everything has been settled."

"I know that," said Alvin, "but is she looking into my mind at this moment?"

The other hesitated.

"No, she isn't," he said at last. "I think she's deliberately leaving you alone, so that her thoughts won't influence you."

That was all he needed to know. For the first time Alvin dared to turn his mind upon the only plan that offered any hope. He was far too stubborn to accept either of the alternatives Seranis had offered him, and even if there had been nothing at stake he would have bitterly resisted any attempt to override his will.

In a little while Seranis would return. He could do nothing until they were in the open again, and even then Seranis would be able to control his actions if he attempted to run away. And apart from that, he was sure

that many of the villagers could intercept him long before
he reached safety.

Very carefully, checking every detail, he traced out
the only road that could lead him back to Diaspar on the
terms he wished.

Theon warned him when Seranis was near, and he
quickly turned his thoughts into harmless channels. It
had never been easy for her to understand his mind, and
now it seemed to Seranis as if she were far out in space,
looking down upon a world veiled with impenetrable
clouds. Sometimes there would be a rift in the covering,
and for an instant she could catch a glimpse of what lay
beneath. She wondered what Alvin was trying to hide
from her. For a moment she dipped into her son's mind,
but Theon knew nothing of the other's plans. She thought
again of the precautions she had taken: as a man may
flex his muscles before some great exertion, she ran
through the compulsion patterns she might have to use.
But there was no trace of her preoccupation as she smiled
at Alvin from the doorway.

"Well," she asked, "have you made up your mind?"

Alvin's reply seemed frank enough.

"Yes," he said. "I will return to Diaspar."

"I'm sorry, and I know that Theon will miss you. But
perhaps it's best: this is not your world and you must
think of your own people."

With a gesture of supreme confidence, she stood aside
to let Alvin pass through the door.

"The men who can obliterate your memory of Lys are
waiting for you: we expected this decision."

Alvin was glad to see that Seranis was leading him in
the direction he wished to go. She did not look back to
see if he was following: her every movement told him:
"Try and run away if you like—my mind is more powerful
than yours." And he knew that it was perfectly true.

They were clear of the houses when he stopped and turned to his friend.

"Good-bye, Theon," he said, holding out his hands. "Thank you for all you've done. One day I'll be back."

Seranis had stopped and was watching him intently. He smiled at her even while he measured the twenty feet of ground between them.

"I know that you're doing this against your will," he said, "and I don't blame you for it. I don't like what I'm doing, either." (That was not true, he thought. Already he was beginning to enjoy himself.) He glanced quickly around: no one was approaching and Seranis had not moved. She was still watching him, probably trying to probe into his mind. He talked quickly to prevent even the outlines of his plan from shaping among his thoughts.

"I do not believe you are right," he said, so unconscious of his intellectual arrogance that Seranis could not resist a smile. "It's wrong for Lys and Diaspar to remain apart forever: one day they may need each other desperately. So I am going home with all that I have learned—*and I do not think that you can stop me.*"

He waited no longer, and it was just as well. Seranis never moved, but instantly he felt his body slipping from his control. The power that had brushed aside his own will was even greater than he had expected, and he realized that many hidden minds must be aiding Seranis. Helplessly he began to walk back towards the center of the village, and for an awful moment he thought his plans had failed.

Then there came a flash of steel and crystal, and the metal arms closed swiftly around him. His body fought against them, as he had known it must do, but his struggles were useless. The ground fell away beneath him and he caught a glimpse of Theon, frozen by surprise with a foolish smile upon his face.

The robot was carrying him a dozen feet above the

ground, much faster than a man could run. It took Seranis only a moment to understand his ruse, and his struggles died away as she relaxed her control. But she was not defeated yet, and presently there happened that which Alvin had feared and done his best to counteract.

There were now two separate entities fighting inside his mind, and one of them was pleading with the robot, begging it to set him down again. The real Alvin waited, breathlessly, resisting only a little against forces he knew he could not hope to fight. He had gambled: there was no way of telling beforehand if the machine could understand orders as complex as those he had given it. Under no circumstances, he had told the robot, must it obey any further commands of his until he was safely inside Diaspar. Those were the orders. If they were obeyed, Alvin had placed his fate beyond the reach of human interference.

Never hesitating, the machine raced on along the path he had so carefully mapped out for it. A part of him was still pleading angrily to be released, but he knew now that he was safe. And presently Seranis understood that too, for the forces inside his brain ceased to war with one another. Once more he was at peace, as ages ago an earlier wanderer had been when, lashed to the mast of his ship, he had heard the song of the Sirens die away across the wine-dark sea.

"So you see," concluded Alvin, "it will carry out any orders I give, no matter how complicated they are. But as soon as I ask questions about its origin, it simply freezes like that."

The machine was hanging motionless above the Master Associator, its crystal lenses glittering in the silver light like a cluster of jewels. Of all the robots which Rorden had ever met, this was by far the most baffling: he was now almost sure that it had been built by no human civilization. With such eternal servants it was not surprising that the Master's personality had survived the ages.

Alvin's return had raised so many problems that Rorden was almost afraid to think of them. He himself had not found it easy to accept the existence of Lys, with all its implications, and he wondered how Diaspar would react to the new knowledge. Probably the city's immense inertia would cushion the shock: it might well be years before all of its inhabitants fully appreciated the fact that they were no longer alone on Earth.

But if Alvin had his way, things would move much more quickly than that. There were times when Rorden regretted the failure of Seranis' plans—everything would have been so much simpler. The problem was immense, and for the second occasion in his life Rorden could not decide what course of action was correct. He wondered how many more times Alvin would present him with such dilemmas, and smiled a little wryly at the thought. For it would make no difference either way: Alvin would do exactly as he pleased.

As yet, not more than a dozen people outside Alvin's own family knew the truth. His parents, with whom he now had so little in common and often did not see for weeks, still seemed to think that he had merely been to some outlying part of the city. Jeserac had been the only person to react strongly: once the initial shock had worn off he had engaged in a violent quarrel with Rorden, and the two were no longer on speaking terms. Alvin, who had seen this coming for some time, could guess the details but to his disappointment neither of the protagonists would talk about the matter.

Later, there would be time enough to see that Diaspar realized the truth: for the moment Alvin was too interested in the robot to worry about much else. He felt, and his belief was now shared by Rorden, that the tale he had heard in Shalmirane was only a fragment of some far greater story. At first Rorden had been skeptical, and he still believed the "Great Ones" to be no more than another of the world's countless religious myths. Only the robot knew the truth, and it had defied a million centuries of questioning as it was defying them now.

"The trouble is," said Rorden, "that there are no longer any engineers left in the world."

Alvin looked puzzled: although contact with the Keeper of the Records had greatly enlarged his vocabulary, there were thousands of archaic words he did not understand.

"An engineer," explained Rorden, "was a man who designed and built machines. It's impossible for us to imagine an age without robots—but every machine in the world had to be invented at one time or other, and until the Master Robots were built they needed men to look after them. Once the machines could care for themselves, human engineers were no longer required. I think that's a fairly accurate account, though of course it's mostly guesswork. Every machine we possess existed at the beginning of our history, and many had disappeared long before it started."

"Such as flyers and spaceships," interjected Alvin.

"Yes," agreed Rorden, "as well as the great communicators that could reach the stars. All these things vanished when they were no longer needed."

Alvin shook his head.

"I still believe," he said, "that the disappearance of the spaceships can't be explained as easily as that. But to get back to the machine—do you think that the Master Robots could help us? I've never seen one, of course, and don't know much about them."

"Help us? In what way?"

"I'm not quite sure," said Alvin vaguely. "Perhaps they could force it to obey *all* my orders. They repair robots, don't they? I suppose that would be a kind of repair. . . ."

His voice faded away as if he had failed even to convince himself.

Rorden smiled: the idea was too ingenuous for him to put much faith in it. However, this piece of historical research was the first of all Alvin's schemes for which he himself could share much enthusiasm, and he could think of no better plan at the moment.

He walked towards the Associator, above which the robot was still floating as if in studied indifference. As he began, almost automatically, to set up his questions on the great keyboard, he was suddenly struck by a thought so incongruous that he burst out laughing.

Alvin looked at his friend in surprise as Rorden turned towards him.

"Alvin," he said between chuckles, "I'm afraid we still have a lot to learn about machines." He laid his hand on the robot's smooth metal body. "They don't share many human feelings, you know. It wasn't really necessary for us to do all our plotting in whispers."

▼

This world, Alvin knew, had not been made for Man. Under the glare of the trichromatic lights—so dazzling that they pained the eyes—the long, broad corridors seemed to stretch to infinity. Down these great passageways all the robots of Diaspar must come at the end of their patient lives, yet not once in a million years had they echoed to the sound of human feet.

It had not been difficult to locate the maps of the underground city, the city of machines without which Diaspar could not exist. A few hundred yards ahead the corridor would open into a circular chamber more than a mile across, its roof supported by great columns that must also bear the unimaginable weight of Power Center. Here, if the maps spoke the truth, the Master Robots, greatest of all machines, kept watch over Diaspar.

The chamber was there, and it was even vaster than Alvin had imagined—but where were the machines? He paused in wonder at the tremendous but meaningless panorama beneath him. The corridor ended high in the wall of the chamber—surely the largest cavity ever built by man—and on either side long ramps swept down to the distant floor. Covering the whole of that brilliantly lit expanse were hundreds of great white structures, so unexpected that for a moment Alvin thought he must be looking down upon a subterranean city. The impression was startlingly vivid and it was one he never wholly lost. Nowhere at all was the sight he had expected—the familiar gleam of metal which since the beginning of time Man had learned to associate with his servants.

Here was the end of an evolution almost as long as Man's. Its beginning was lost in the mists of the Dawn Ages, when humanity had first learned the use of power and sent its noisy engines clanking about the world.

Steam, water, wind—all had been harnessed for a little while and then abandoned. For centuries the energy of matter had run the world until it too had been superseded, and with each change the old machines were forgotten and the new ones took their place. Very slowly, over millions of years, the ideal of the perfect machine was approached—that ideal which had once been a dream, then a distant prospect, and at last reality:

No machine may contain any moving parts.

Here was the ultimate expression of that ideal. Its achievement had taken Man perhaps a thousand million years, and in the hour of his triumph he had turned his back upon the machine forever.

The robot they were seeking was not as large as many of its companions, but Alvin and Rorden felt dwarfed when they stood beneath it. The five tiers with their sweeping horizontal lines gave the impression of some crouching beast, and looking from it to his own robot Alvin thought it strange that the same word should be used for both.

Almost three feet from the ground a wide transparent panel ran the whole length of the structure. Alvin pressed his forehead against the smooth, curiously warm material and peered into the machine. At first he saw nothing: then, by shielding his eyes, he could distinguish thousands of faint points of light hanging in nothingness. They were ranged one beyond the other in a three-dimensional lattice, as strange and as meaningless to him as the stars must have been to ancient Man.

Rorden had joined him and together they stared into the brooding monster. Though they watched for many minutes, the colored lights never moved from their places and their brilliance never changed. Presently Alvin broke away from the machine and turned to his friend.

"What are they?" he asked in perplexity.

"If we could look into our own minds," said Rorden,

"they would mean as little to us. The robots seem motionless because we cannot see their thoughts."

For the first time Alvin looked at the long avenue of titans with some trace of understanding. All his life he had accepted without question the miracle of the synthesizers, the machines which age after age produced in an unending stream all that the city needed. Thousands of times he had watched that act of creation, never thinking that somewhere must exist the prototype of that which he had seen come into the world.

As a human mind may dwell for a little while upon a single thought, so these greater brains could grasp and hold forever the most intricate ideas. The patterns of all created things were frozen in these eternal minds, needing only the touch of a human will to make them reality.

The world had gone very far since, hour upon hour, the first cavemen had patiently chipped their arrowheads and knives from the stubborn stone.

"Our problem now," said Rorden, "is to get into touch with the creature. It can never have any direct knowledge of Man, for there's no way in which we can affect its consciousness. If my information's correct, there must be an interpreting machine somewhere. That was a type of robot that could convert human instructions into commands that the Master Robots could understand. They were pure intelligence with little memory—just as this is a tremendous memory with relatively little intelligence."

Alvin considered for a moment. Then he pointed to his own robot.

"Why not use it?" he suggested. "Robots have very literal minds. It won't refuse to pass on our instructions, for I doubt if the Master ever thought of this situation."

Rorden laughed.

"I don't suppose he did, but since there's a machine specially built for the job I think it would be best to use it."

The Interpreter was a very small affair, a horseshoe-shaped construction built round a vision screen which lit up as they approached. Of all the machines in this great cavern, it was the only one which had shown any cognizance of Man, and its greeting seemed a little contemptuous. For on the screen appeared the words:

> STATE YOUR PROBLEM
> PLEASE THINK CLEARLY

Ignoring the implied insult, Alvin began his story. Though he had communicated with robots by speech or thought on countless occasions, he felt now that he was addressing something more than a machine. Lifeless though this creature was, it possessed an intelligence that might be greater than his own. It was a strange thought, but it did not depress him unduly—for of what use was intelligence alone?

His words died away and the silence of that overpowering place crowded back upon them. For a moment the screen was filled with swirling mist: then the haze cleared and the machine replied:

> REPAIR IMPOSSIBLE
> ROBOT UNKNOWN TYPE

Alvin turned to his friend with a gesture of disappointment, but even as he did so the lettering changed and a second message appeared:

> DUPLICATION COMPLETED
> PLEASE CHECK AND SIGN

Simultaneously a red light began to flash above a horizontal panel Alvin had not noticed before, and was certain he must have seen had it been there earlier. Puzzled, he bent towards it, but a shout from Rorden made him look round in surprise. The other was pointing towards the great Master Robot, where Alvin had left his own machine a few minutes before.

It had not moved, but it had multiplied. Hanging in the air beside it was a duplicate so exact that Alvin could not tell which was the original and which the copy.

"I was watching when it happened," said Rorden excitedly. "It suddenly seemed to extend, as if millions of replicas had come into existence on either side of it. Then all the images except these two disappeared. The one on the right is the original."

Alvin was still stunned, but slowly he began to realize what must have happened. His robot could not be forced to disobey the orders given it so long ago, but a duplicate could be made with all its knowledge yet with the unbreakable memory-block removed. Beautiful though the solution was, the mind would be unwise to dwell too long upon the powers that made it possible.

The robots moved as one when Alvin called them towards him. Speaking his commands, as he often did for Rorden's benefit, he asked again the question he had put so many times in different forms.

"Can you tell me how your first master reached Shalmirane?"

Rorden wished his mind could intercept the soundless replies, of which he had never been able to catch even a fragment. But this time there was little need, for the glad smile that spread across Alvin's face was sufficient answer.

The boy looked at him triumphantly.

"Number One is just the same," he said, "but Two is willing to talk."

"I think we should wait until we're home again before we begin to ask questions," said Rorden, practical as ever. "We'll need the Associators and Recorders when we start."

Impatient though he was, Alvin had to admit the wisdom of the advice. As he turned to go, Rorden smiled at his eagerness and said quietly:

"Haven't you forgotten something?"

The red light on the Interpreter was still flashing, and its message still glowed on the screen.

PLEASE CHECK AND SIGN

Alvin walked to the machine and examined the panel above which the light was blinking. Set in it was a window of some almost invisible substance, supporting a stylus which passed vertically through it. The point of the stylus rested on a sheet of white material which already bore several signatures and dates. The last of them was almost fifty thousand years ago, and Alvin recognized the name as that of a recent President of the Council. Above it only two other names were visible, neither of which meant anything to him or to Rorden. Nor was this very surprising, for they had been written twenty-three and fifty-seven million years before.

Alvin could see no purpose for this ritual, but he knew that he could never fathom the workings of the minds that had built this place. With a slight feeling of unreality he grasped the stylus and began to write his name. The instrument seemed completely free to move in the horizontal plane, for in that direction the window offered no more resistance than the wall of a soap-bubble. Yet his full strength was incapable of moving it vertically: he knew, because he tried.

Carefully he wrote the date and released the stylus. It moved slowly back across the sheet to its original position —and the panel with its winking light was gone.

As Alvin walked away, he wondered why his predecessors had come here and what they had sought from the machine. No doubt, thousands or millions of years in the future, other men would look into that panel and ask themselves: "Who was Alvin of Loronei?" *Or would they?* Perhaps they would exclaim instead: "Look! Here's Alvin's signature!"

The thought was not untypical of him in his present

mood, but he knew better than to share it with his friend.

At the entrance to the corridor they looked back across the cave, and the illusion was stronger than ever. Lying beneath them was a dead city of strange white buildings, a city bleached by the fierce light not meant for human eyes. Dead it might be, for it had never lived, but Alvin knew that when Diaspar had passed away these machines would still be here, never turning their minds from the thoughts greater men than he had given them long ago.

They spoke little on the way back through the streets of Diaspar, streets bathed with sunlight which seemed pale and wan after the glare of the machine city. Each in his own way was thinking of the knowledge that would soon be his, and neither had any regard for the beauty of the great towers drifting past, or the curious glances of their fellow citizens.

It was strange, thought Alvin, how everything that had happened to him led up to this moment. He knew well enough that men were makers of their own destinies, yet since he had met Rorden events seemed to have moved automatically towards a predetermined goal. Alaine's message—Lys—Shalmirane—at every stage he might have turned aside with unseeing eyes, but something had led him on. It was pleasant to pretend that Fate had favoured him, but his rational mind knew better. Any man might have found the path his footsteps had traced, and countless times in the past ages others must have gone almost as far. He was simply the first to be lucky.

The first to be lucky. The words echoed mockingly in his ears as they stepped through the door of Rorden's chamber. Quietly waiting for them, with hands folded patiently across his lap, was a man wearing a curious garb unlike any that Alvin had ever seen before. He glanced enquiringly at Rorden, and was instantly shocked by the pallor of his friend's face. Then he knew who the visitor was.

He rose as they entered and made a stiff, formal bow. Without a word he handed a small cylinder to Rorden, who took it woodenly and broke the seal. The almost un-heard-of rarity of a written message made the silent ex-change doubly impressive. When he had finished Rorden returned the cylinder with another slight bow, at which, in spite of his anxiety, Alvin could not resist a smile.

Rorden appeared to have recovered himself quickly, for when he spoke his voice was perfectly normal.

"It seems that the Council would like a word with us, Alvin. I'm afraid we've kept it waiting."

Alvin had guessed as much. The crisis had come sooner—much sooner—than he had expected. He was not, he told himself, afraid of the Council, but the interruption was maddening. His eyes strayed involuntarily to the ro-bots.

"You'll have to leave them behind," said Rorden firmly.

Their eyes met and clashed. Then Alvin glanced at the Messenger.

"Very well," he said quietly.

The party was very silent on its way to the Council Chamber. Alvin was marshalling the arguments he had never properly thought out, believing they would not be needed for many years. He was far more annoyed than alarmed, and he felt angry at himself for being so unpre-pared.

They waited only a few minutes in the anteroom, but it was long enough for Alvin to wonder why, if he was unafraid, his legs felt so curiously weak. Then the great doors contracted, and they walked towards the twenty men gathered round their famous table.

This, Alvin knew, was the first Council Meeting in his lifetime, and he felt a little flattered as he noticed that there were no empty seats. He had never known that

Jeserac was a Council member. At his startled gaze the old man shifted uneasily in his chair and gave him a furtive smile as if to say: "This is nothing to do with me." Most of the other faces Alvin had expected, and only two were quite unknown to him.

The President began to address them in a friendly voice, and looking at the familiar faces before him, Alvin could see no great cause for Rorden's alarm. His confidence began to return: Rorden, he decided, was something of a coward. In that he did his friend less than justice, for although courage had never been one of Rorden's most conspicuous qualities, his worry concerned his ancient office almost as much as himself. Never in history had a Keeper of the Records been relieved of his position: Rorden was very anxious not to create a precedent.

In the few minutes since he had entered the Council Chamber, Alvin's plans had undergone a remarkable change. The speech he had so carefully rehearsed was forgotten: the fine phrases he had been practising were reluctantly discarded. To his support now had come his most treacherous ally—that sense of the ridiculous which had always made it impossible for him to take very seriously even the most solemn occasions. The Council might meet once in a thousand years: it might control the destinies of Diaspar—but those who sat upon it were only tired old men. Alvin knew Jeserac, and he did not believe that the others would be very different. He felt a disconcerting pity for them and suddenly remembered the words Seranis had spoken to him in Lys: "Ages ago we sacrificed our immortality, but Diaspar still follows the false dream." That in truth these men had done, and he did not believe it had brought them happiness.

So when at the President's invitation Alvin began to describe his journey to Lys, he was to all appearances no more than a boy who had by chance stumbled on a discovery he thought of little importance. There was no hint of any plan or deeper purpose: only natural curiosity had led him out of Diaspar. It might have happened to anyone, yet he contrived to give the impression that he expected a little praise for his cleverness. Of Shalmirane and the robots, he said nothing at all.

It was quite a good performance, though Alvin was the only person who could fully appreciate it. The Council as a whole seemed favourably impressed, but Jeserac wore an expression in which relief struggled with incredulity. At Rorden, Alvin dared not look.

When he had quite finished, there was a brief silence while the Council considered his statement. Then the President spoke again:

"We fully appreciate," he said, choosing his words with obvious care, "that you had the best of motives in what you did. However, you have created a somewhat difficult situation for us. Are you quite sure that your discovery was accidental, and that no one, shall we say, *influenced* you in any way?" His eyes wandered thoughtfully towards Rorden.

For the last time, Alvin yielded to the mischievous promptings of his mind.

"I wouldn't say that," he replied, after an appearance of considerable thought. There was a sudden quickening of interest among the Council members, and Rorden stirred uneasily by his side. Alvin gave his audience a smile that lacked nothing of candor, and added quickly in a guileless voice:

"I'm sure I owe a great deal to my tutor."

At this unexpected and singularly misleading compliment, all eyes were turned upon Jeserac, who became a deep red, started to speak, and then thought better of it. There was an awkward silence until the President stepped into the breach.

"Thank you," he said hastily. "You will remain here while we consider your statement."

There was an audible sigh of relief from Rorden—and that was the last sound Alvin heard for some time. A blanket of silence had descended upon him, and although he could see the Council arguing heatedly, not a word of its deliberations reached him. It was amusing at first, but the spectacle soon became tedious and he was glad when the silence lifted again.

"We have come to the conclusion," said the President, "that there has been an unfortunate mishap for which no one can be held responsible—although we consider that the Keeper of the Records should have informed us sooner of what was happening. However, it is perhaps as well that this dangerous discovery has been made, for we can now take suitable steps to prevent its recurrence. We will deal ourselves with the transport system you have located, and you"—turning to Rorden for the first time— "will ensure that all references to Lys are removed from the Records."

There was a murmur of applause and expressions of satisfaction spread across the faces of the councillors. A difficult situation had been speedily dealt with, they had avoided the unpleasant necessity of reprimanding Rorden, and now they could go their ways again feeling that they, the chief citizens of Diaspar, had done their duty. With reasonably good fortune it might be centuries before the need arose again.

Even Rorden, disappointed though he was for Alvin's sake as well as his own, felt relieved at the outcome. Things might have been very much worse—

A voice he had never heard before cut into his reverie and froze the councillors in their seats, the complacent smiles slowly ebbing from their faces.

"And precisely why are you going to close the way to Lys?"

It was some time before Rorden's mind, unwilling to

recognize disater, would admit that it was Alvin who spoke.

The success of his subterfuge had given Alvin only a moment's satisfaction. Throughout the President's address his anger had been steadily rising as he realized that, despite all his cleverness, his plans were to be thwarted. The feelings he had known in Lys when Seranis had presented her ultimatum came back with redoubled strength. He had won that contest, and the taste of power was still sweet.

This time he had no robot to help him, and he did not know what the outcome would be. But he no longer had any fear of these foolish old men who thought themselves the rulers of Diaspar. He had seen the real rulers of the city, and had spoken to them in the grave silence of their brilliant, buried world. So in his anger and arrogance, Alvin threw away his disguise and the councillors looked in vain for the artless boy who had addressed them a little while ago.

"Why are you going to close the way to Lys?"

There was silence in the Council Room, but the lips of Jeserac twisted into a slow, secret smile. This Alvin was new to him, but it was less alien than the one who had spoken before.

The President chose at first to ignore the challenge. Perhaps he could not bring himself to believe that it was more than an innocent question, however violently it had been expressed.

"That is a matter of high policy which we cannot discuss here," he said pompously, "but Diaspar cannot risk contamination with other cultures." He gave Alvin a benevolent but slightly worried smile.

"It's rather strange," said Alvin coldly, "that in Lys I was told exactly the same thing about Diaspar." He was glad to see the start of annoyance, but gave his audience no time to reply.

"Lys," he continued, "is much larger than Diaspar and its culture is certainly not inferior. It's always known about us but has chosen not to reveal itself—as you put it, to avoid contamination. Isn't it obvious that we are *both* wrong?"

He looked expectantly along the lines of faces, but nowhere was there any understanding of his words. Suddenly his anger against these leaden-eyed old men rose to a crescendo. The blood was throbbing in his cheeks, and though his voice was steadier now it held a note of icy contempt which even the most pacific of the councillors could no longer overlook.

"Our ancestors," began Alvin, "built an empire which reached to the stars. Men came and went at will among all those worlds—and now their descendants are afraid to stir beyond the walls of their city. *Shall I tell you why?*" He paused: there was no movement at all in the great bare room.

"It is because we are afraid—afraid of something that happened at the beginning of history. I was told the truth in Lys, though I had guessed it long ago. Must we always hide like cowards in Diaspar, pretending that nothing else exists—because half a billion years ago the Invaders drove us back to Earth?"

He had put his finger on their secret fear, the fear that he had never shared and whose power he could therefore never understand. Let them do what they pleased: he had spoken the truth.

His anger drained away and he was himself again, as yet only a little alarmed at what he had done. He turned to the President in a last gesture of independence.

"Have I your permission to leave?"

Still no words were spoken, but the slight inclination of the head gave him his release. The great doors expanded before him and not until long after they had closed again did the storm break upon the Council Chamber.

The President waited until the inevitable lull. Then he turned to Jeserac.

"It seems to me," he said, "that we should hear your views first."

Jeserac examined the remark for possible traps. Then he replied:

"I think that Diaspar is now losing its most outstanding brain."

"What do you mean?"

"Isn't it obvious? By now young Alvin will be halfway to the Tomb of Yarlan Zey. No, we shouldn't interfere. I shall be very sorry to lose him, though he never cared very much for me." He sighed a little. "For that matter, he never cared a great deal for anyone save Alvin of Loronei."

Not until an hour later was Rorden able to escape from
the Council Chamber. The delay was maddening, and
when he reached his rooms he knew it was too late. He
paused at the entrance, wondering if Alvin had left any
message, and realizing for the first time how empty the
years ahead would be.

The message was there, but its contents were totally
unexpected. Even when Rorden had read it several times,
he was still completely baffled:

"Meet me at once in the Tower of Loranne."

Only once before had he been to the Tower of Loranne,
when Alvin had dragged him there to watch the sunset.
That was years ago: the experience had been unforget-
table but the shadow of night sweeping across the desert
had terrified him so much that he had fled, pursued by
Alvin's entreaties. He had sworn that he would never go
there again. . . .

Yet here he was, in that bleak chamber pierced with
the horizontal ventilating shafts. There was no sign of
Alvin, but when he called, the boy's voice answered at
once.

"I'm on the parapet—come through the center shaft."

Rorden hesitated: there were many things he would
much rather do. But a moment later he was standing beside Alvin with his back to the city and the desert stretch-
ing endlessly before him.

They looked at each other in silence for a little while.
Then Alvin said, rather contritely:

"I hope I didn't get you into trouble."

Rorden was touched, and many truths he was about to utter died abruptly on his lips. Instead he replied:

"The Council was too busy arguing with itself to bother about me." He chuckled. "Jeserac was putting up quite a spirited defense when I left. I'm afraid I misjudged him."

"I'm sorry about Jeserac."

"Perhaps it was an unkind trick to play on the old man, but I think he's rather enjoying himself. After all, there was some truth in your remark. He was the first man to show you the ancient world, and he has rather a guilty conscience."

For the first time, Alvin smiled.

"It's strange," he said, "but until I lost my temper I never really understood what I wanted to do. Whether they like it or not, I'm going to break down the wall between Diaspar and Lys. But that can wait: it's no longer so important now."

Rorden felt a little alarmed.

"What do you mean?" he asked anxiously. For the first time he noticed that only one of the robots was with them on the parapet. "Where's the second machine?"

Slowly Alvin raised his arm and pointed out across the desert, towards the broken hills and the long line of sand dunes, crisscrossed like frozen waves. Far away, Rorden could see the unmistakable gleam of sunlight upon metal.

"We've been waiting for you," said Alvin quietly. "As soon as I left the Council, I went straight to the robots. Whatever happened, I was going to make sure that no one took them away before I'd learnt all they could teach me. It didn't take long, for they're not very intelligent and knew less than I'd hoped. *But I have found the secret of the Master.*" He paused for a moment, then pointed again at the almost invisible robot. "Watch!"

The glistening speck soared away from the desert and

came to rest perhaps a thousand feet above the ground. At first, not knowing what to expect, Rorden could see no other change. Then, scarcely believing his eyes, he saw that a cloud of dust was slowly rising from the desert.

Nothing is more terrible than movement where no movement should ever be again, but Rorden was beyond surprise or fear when the great sand dunes began to slide apart. Beneath the desert something was stirring like a giant awaking from its sleep, and presently there came to Rorden's ears the rumble of falling earth and the shriek of rock split asunder by irresistible force. Then, suddenly, a great geyser of sand erupted hundreds of feet into the air and the ground was hidden from sight.

Slowly the dust began to settle back into the jagged wound torn across the face of the desert. But Rorden and Alvin still kept their eyes fixed steadfastly upon the open sky, which a little while ago had held only the waiting robot. What Alvin was thinking, Rorden could scarcely imagine. At last he knew what the boy had meant when he had said that nothing else was very important now. The great city behind them and the greater desert before, the timidity of the Council and the pride of Lys—all these seemed trivial matters now.

The covering of earth and rock could blur but could not conceal the proud lines of the ship still ascending from the riven desert. As Rorden watched, it slowly turned towards them until it had foreshortened to a circle. Then, very leisurely, the circle started to expand.

Alvin began to speak, rather quickly, as if the time were short.

"I still do not know who the Master was, or why he came to Earth. The robot gives me the impression that he landed secretly and hid his ship where it could be easily found if he ever needed it again. In all the world there could have been no better hiding place than the

Port of Diaspar, which now lies beneath those sands and which even in his age must have been utterly deserted. He may have lived for a while in Diaspar before he went to Shalmirane: the road must still have been open in those days. But he never needed the ship again, and all these ages it has been waiting out there beneath the sands."

The ship was now very close, as the controlling robot guided it towards the parapet. Rorden could see that it was about a hundred feet long and sharply pointed at both ends. There appeared to be no windows or other openings, though the thick layer of earth made it impossible to be certain.

Suddenly they were spattered with dirt as a section of the hull opened outwards, and Rorden caught a glimpse of a small, bare room with a second door at its far end. The ship was now hanging only a foot away from the parapet, which it had approached very cautiously like a sensitive, living thing. Rorden had backed away from it as if he were afraid, which indeed was very near the truth. To him the ship symbolized all the terror and mystery of the Universe, and evoked as could no other object the racial fears which for so long had paralyzed the will of the human race. Looking at his friend, Alvin knew very well the thoughts that were passing through his brain. For almost the first time he realized that there were forces in men's minds over which they had no control, and that the Council was deserving of pity rather than contempt.

In utter silence, the ship drew away from the tower. It was strange, Rorden thought, that for the second time in his life he had said good-bye to Alvin. The little, closed world of Diaspar knew only one farewell, and that was for eternity.

The ship was now only a dark stain against the sky, and

of a sudden Rorden lost it altogether. He never saw its going, but presently there echoed down from the heavens the most awe-inspiring of all the sounds that Man had ever made—the long-drawn thunder of air falling, mile after mile, into a tunnel drilled suddenly across the sky.

Even when the last echoes had died away into the desert, Rorden never moved. He was thinking of the boy who had gone—wondering, as he had so often done, if he would ever understand that aloof and baffling mind. Alvin would never grow up: to him the whole Universe was a plaything, a puzzle to be unravelled for his own amusement. In his play he had now found the ultimate, deadly toy which might wreck what was left of human civilization—but whatever the outcome, to him it would still be a game.

The sun was now low on the horizon, and a chill wind was blowing from the desert. But still Rorden waited, conquering his fears, and presently for the first time in his life he saw the stars.

Even in Diaspar, Alvin had never seen such luxury as that which lay before him when the inner door of the airlock slid aside. At first he did not understand its implications: then he began to wonder, rather uneasily, how long this tiny world might be upon its journeying between the stars. There were no controls of any kind, but the large, oval screen which completely covered the far wall would have shown that this was no ordinary room. Ranged in a half-circle before it were three low couches: the rest of the cabin was occupied by two tables, a number of most inviting chairs, and many curious devices which for the moment Alvin could not identify.

When he had made himself comfortable in front of the screen, he looked around for the robots. To his surprise, they had disappeared: then he located them, neatly stowed away in recesses high up beneath the curved ceiling. Their action had been so completely natural that Alvin knew at once the purpose for which they had been intended. He remembered the Master Robots: these were the Interpreters, without which no untrained human mind could control a machine as complex as a spaceship. They had brought the Master to Earth and then, as his servants, followed him into Lys. Now they were ready, as if the intervening eons had never been, to carry out their old duties once again.

Alvin threw them an experimental command, and the great screen shivered into life. Before him was the Tower of Loranne, curiously foreshortened and apparently lying on its side. Further trials gave him views of the sky, of the city, and of great expanses of desert. The definition was brilliantly, almost unnaturally, clear, although there seemed to be no actual magnification. Alvin wondered if the ship itself moved as the picture changed, but could think of no way of discovering this. He experimented for a little while until he could obtain any view he wished: then he was ready to start.

"Take me to Lys"—the command was a simple one, but how could the ship obey it when he himself had no idea of the direction? Alvin had never thought of this, and when it did occur to him the machine was already moving across the desert at a tremendous speed. He shrugged his shoulders, thankfully accepting what he could not understand.

It was difficult to judge the scale of the picture racing up the screen, but many miles must be passing every minute. Not far from the city the color of the ground had changed abruptly to a dull grey, and Alvin knew that he was now passing over the bed of one of the lost oceans. Once Diaspar must have been very near the sea, though there had never been any hint of this even in the most ancient records. Old though the city was, the oceans must have passed away long before its building.

Hundreds of miles later, the ground rose sharply and the desert returned. Once Alvin halted his ship above a curious pattern of intersecting lines, showing faintly through the blanket of sand. For a moment it puzzled him: then he realized that he was looking down on the ruins of some forgotten city. He did not stay for long: it was heartbreaking to think that billions of men had left no other trace of their existence save these furrows in the sand.

The smooth curve of the horizon was breaking up at last, crinkling into mountains that were beneath him almost as soon as they were glimpsed. The machine was slowing now, slowing and falling to earth in a great arc a hundred miles in length. And then below him was Lys, its forests and endless rivers forming a scene of such incomparable beauty that for a while he would go no farther. To the east, the land was shadowed and the great lakes floated upon it like pools of darker night. But towards the sunset, the waters danced and sparkled with light, throwing back towards him such colors as he had never imagined.

It was not difficult to locate Airlee—which was fortunate, for the robots could guide him no farther. Alvin had expected this, and felt glad to have discovered some limits to their powers. After a little experimenting, he brought his ship to rest on the hillside which had given him his first glimpse of Lys. It was quite easy to control the machine: he had only to indicate his general desires and the robots attended to the details. They would, he imagined, probably ignore any dangerous or impossible orders, but he did not intend to try the experiment.

Alvin was fairly certain that no one could have seen his arrival. He thought this rather important, for he had no desire to engage in mental combat with Seranis again.

His plans were still somewhat vague, but he was running no risks until he had re-established friendly relations.

The discovery that the original robot would no longer obey him was a considerable shock. When he ordered it from its little compartment it refused to move but lay motionless, watching him dispassionately with its multiple eyes. To Alvin's relief, the replica obeyed him instantly, but no amount of cajoling could make the prototype carry out even the simplest action. Alvin worried for some time before the explanation of the mutiny occurred to him. For all their wonderful skills, the robots were not very intelligent, and the events of the past hour must have been too much for the unfortunate machine. One by one it had seen all the Master's orders defied—those orders which it had obeyed with such singleness of purpose for so many millions of years.

It was too late for regrets now, but Alvin was sorry he had made only a single duplicate. For the borrowed robot had become insane.

Alvin met no one on the road to Airlee. It was strange to sit in the spaceship while his field of vision moved effortlessly along the familiar path and the whispering of the forest sounded in his ears. As yet he was unable to identify himself fully with the robot, and the strain of controlling it was still considerable.

It was nearly dark when he reached Airlee, and the little houses were floating in pools of light. Alvin kept to the shadows and had almost reached Seranis' home before he was discovered. Suddenly there was an angry, high-pitched buzzing and his view was blocked by a flurry of wings. He recoiled involuntarily before the onslaught: then he realized what had happened. Krif did not approve of anything that flew without wings, and only Theon's presence had prevented him from attacking the robot on earlier occasions. Not wishing to hurt the beautiful but stupid creature, Alvin brought the robot to a halt and endured as best he could the blows that seemed to be raining upon him. Though he was sitting in comfort a mile away, he could not avoid flinching and was glad when Theon came out to investigate.

At his master's approach Krif departed, still buzzing balefully. In the silence that followed Theon stood looking at the robot for a while. Then he smiled.

"I'm glad you've come back. Or are you still in Diaspar?"

Not for the first time Alvin felt a twinge of envy as he realized how much quicker Theon's mind was than his own.

"No," he said, wondering as he did so how clearly the robot echoed his voice. "I'm in Airlee, not very far away. But I'm staying here for the present."

Theon laughed heartily.

"I think that's just as well," he said. "Mother's forgiven you, but the Central Council hasn't. There's a conference going on indoors now: I have to keep out of the way."

"What are they talking about?"

"I'm not supposed to know, but they asked me all sorts of questions about you. I had to tell them what happened in Shalmirane."

"That doesn't matter very much," replied Alvin. "A good many other things have happened since then. I'd like to have a talk with this Central Council of yours."

"Oh, the whole Council isn't here, naturally. But three of its members have been making enquiries ever since you left."

Alvin smiled. He could well believe it: wherever he went now he seemed to be leaving a trail of consternation behind him.

The comfort and security of the spaceship gave him a confidence he had seldom known before, and he felt complete master of the situation as he followed Theon into the house. The door of the conference room was locked and it was some time before Theon could attract attention. Then the walls slid reluctantly apart, and Alvin moved his robot swiftly forward into the chamber.

The room was the familiar one in which he had had his last interview with Seranis. Overhead the stars were twinkling as if there were no ceiling or upper floor, and once again Alvin wondered how the illusion was achieved. The three councillors froze in their seats as he floated towards them, but only the slightest flicker of surprise crossed Seranis' face.

"Good evening," he said politely, as if this vicarious entry were the most natural thing in the world. "I've decided to come back."

Their surprise exceeded his expectations. One of the councillors, a young man with greying hair, was the first to recover.

"How did you get here?" he gasped.

Alvin thought it wise to evade the question: the way in which it was asked made him suspicious and he wondered if the underground transport system had been put out of action.

"Why, just as I did last time," he lied.

Two of the councillors looked fixedly at the third, who spread his hands in a gesture of baffled resignation. Then the young man who had addressed him before spoke again.

"Didn't you have any—difficulty?"

"None at all," said Alvin, determined to increase their confusion. He saw that he had succeeded.

"I've come back," he continued, "under my own free will, but in view of our previous disagreement I'm remaining out of sight for the moment. If I appear personally, will you promise not to try and restrict my movements again?"

No one said anything for a while and Alvin wondered what thoughts were being exchanged. Then Seranis spoke for them all.

"I imagine that there is little purpose in doing so. Diaspar must know all about us by now."

Alvin flushed slightly at the reproach in her voice.

"Yes, Diaspar knows," he replied. "And Diaspar will have nothing to do with you. It wishes to avoid contamination with an inferior culture."

It was most satisfying to watch the councillors' reactions, and even Seranis colored slightly at his words. If he could make Lys and Diaspar sufficiently annoyed with each other, Alvin realized that his problem would be more than half solved. He was learning, still unconsciously, the lost art of politics.

"But I don't want to stay out here all night," he continued. "Have I your promise?"

Seranis sighed, and a faint smile played about her lips.

"Yes," she said, "We won't attempt to control you again. Though I don't think we were very successful before."

Alvin waited until the robot had returned. Very carefully he gave the machine its instructions and made it repeat them back. Then he left the ship, and the airlock closed silently behind him.

There was a faint whisper of air but no other sound. For a moment a dark shadow blotted out the stars: then the ship was gone. Not until it had vanished did Alvin realize his miscalculation. He had forgotten that the robot's senses were very different from his own, and the night was far darker than he had expected. More than once he lost the path completely, and several times he barely avoided colliding with trees. It was blackest of all in the forest, and once something quite large came towards him through the undergrowth. There was the faintest crackling of twigs, and two emerald eyes were looking steadfastly at him from the level of his waist. He called softly, and an incredibly long tongue rasped across his hand. A moment later a powerful body rubbed affectionately against him and departed without a sound. He had no idea what it could be.

Presently the lights of the village were shining through the trees ahead, but he no longer needed their guidance, for the path beneath his feet had now become a river of dim blue fire. The moss upon which he was walking was luminous and his footprints left dark patches which slowly disappeared behind him. It was a beautiful and entrancing sight, and when Alvin stooped to pluck some of the strange moss it glowed for minutes in his cupped hands before its radiance died.

Theon was waiting for him outside the house, and for the second time he was introduced to the three councillors. He noticed with some annoyance their barely concealed surprise: not appreciating the unfair advantages it gave him, he never cared to be reminded of his youth.

They said little while he refreshed himself, and Alvin wondered what mental notes were being compared. He kept his mind as empty as he could until he had finished: then he began to talk as he had never talked before.

His theme was Diaspar. He painted the city as he had last seen it, dreaming on the breast of the desert, its towers glowing like captive rainbows against the sky. From the treasure-house of memory he recalled the songs that the poets of old had written in praise of Diaspar, and he spoke of the countless men who had burnt away their lives to increase its beauty. No one now, he told them, could ever exhaust a hundredth of the city's treasures, however long they lived. For a while he described some of the wonders which the men of Diaspar had wrought: he tried to make them catch a glimpse at least of the loveliness which such artists as Shervane and Perildor had created for men's eternal admiration. And he spoke also of Loronei, whose name he bore, and wondered a little wistfully if it were indeed true that his music was the last sound Earth had ever broadcast to the stars.

They heard him to the end without interruption or questioning. When he had finished it was very late and Alvin felt more tired than he could ever remember. The strain and excitement of the long day had told on him at last, and quite suddenly he fell asleep.

Alvin was still tired when they left the village not long after dawn. Early though it was, they were not the first upon the road. By the lake they overtook the three councillors, and both parties exchanged slightly self-conscious greetings. Alvin knew perfectly well where the Committee of Investigation was going, and thought it would be appreciated if he saved it some trouble. He stopped when they reached the foot of the hill and turned towards his companions.

"I'm afraid I misled you last night," he said cheerfully. "I didn't come to Lys by the old route, so your attempt to close it wasn't really necessary."

The councillors' faces were a study in relief and increased perplexity.

"Then how *did* you get here?" The leader of the Committee spoke, and Alvin could tell that he at least had begun to guess the truth. He wondered if he had intercepted the command his mind had just sent winging across the mountains. But he said nothing, and merely pointed in silence to the northern sky.

Too swift for the eye to follow, a needle of silver light arced across the mountains, leaving a mile-long trail of incandescence. Twenty thousand feet above Lys, it stopped. There was no deceleration, no slow braking of its colossal speed. It came to a halt instantly, so that the eye that had been following it moved on across a quarter of the heavens before the brain could arrest its motion. Down from the skies crashed a mighty peal of thunder, the sound of air battered and smashed by the violence of the ship's passage. A little later the ship itself, gleaming splendidly in the sunlight, came to rest upon the hillside a hundred yards away.

It was difficult to say who was the most surprised, but Alvin was the first to recover. As they walked—very nearly running—towards the spaceship, he wondered if it normally travelled in this abrupt fashion. The thought was disconcerting, although there had been no sensation of movement on his first voyage. Considerably more puzzling, however, was the fact that the day before this resplendent creature had been hidden beneath a thick layer of iron-hard rock. Not until Alvin had reached the ship, and burnt his fingers by incautiously resting them on the hull, did he understand what had happened. Near the stern there were still traces of earth, but it had been fused into lava. All the rest had been swept away, leaving uncovered the stubborn metal which neither time nor any natural force could ever touch.

With Theon by his side, Alvin stood in the open door and looked back at the three silent councillors. He wondered what they were thinking, but their expressions gave no hint of their thoughts.

"I have a debt to pay in Shalmirane," he said. "Please tell Seranis we'll be back by noon."

The councillors watched until the ship, now moving quite slowly—for it had only a little way to go—had disappeared into the south. Then the young man who led the group shrugged his shoulders philosophically.

"You've always opposed us for wanting change," he said, "and so far you've won. But I don't think the future lies with either of our parties now. Lys and Diaspar have both come to the end of an era, and we must make the best of it."

There was silence for a little while. Then one of his companions spoke in a very thoughtful voice.

"I know nothing of archaeology, but surely that machine was too large to be an ordinary flyer. Do you think it could possibly have been—"

"A spaceship? If so, this *is* a crisis!"

The third man had also been thinking deeply.

"The disappearance of both flyers and spaceships is one of the greatest mysteries of the Interregnum. That machine may be either: for the moment we had better assume the worst. If it is in fact a spaceship, we must at all costs prevent that boy from leaving Earth. There is the danger that he may attract the Invaders again. That would be the end."

A gloomy silence settled over the company until the leader spoke again.

"That machine came from Diaspar," he said slowly. "Someone there must know the truth. I think we had better get in touch with our cousins—if they'll condescend to speak to us."

Sooner than he had any right to expect, the seed that Alvin had planted was beginning to flower.

The mountains were still swimming in shadow when they reached Shalmirane. From their height the great bowl of the fortress looked very small: it seemed impossible that the fate of Earth had once depended on that tiny ebon disc.

When Alvin brought the ship to rest among the ruins, the desolation crowded upon him, chilling his soul. There was no sign of the old man or his machines, and they had some difficulty in finding the entrance to the tunnel. At the top of the stairway Alvin shouted to give warning of their arrival: there was no reply and they moved quietly forward, in case he was asleep.

Sleeping he was, his hands folded peacefully upon his breast. His eyes were open, staring sightlessly up at the massive roof, as if they could see through to the stars beyond. There was a slight smile upon his lips: Death had not come to him as an enemy.

The two robots were beside him, floating motionless in the air. When Alvin tried to approach the body, their tentacles reached out to restrain him, so he came no nearer. There was nothing he could do: as he stood in that silent room he felt an icy wind sweep through his heart. It was the first time he had looked upon the marble face of Death, and he knew that something of his childhood had passed forever.

So this was the end of that strange brotherhood, perhaps the last of its kind the world would know. Deluded though they might have been, these men's lives had not been wholly wasted. As if by a miracle they had saved from the past knowledge that else would have been lost forever. Now their order could go the way of a million other faiths that had once thought themselves eternal.

They left him sleeping in his tomb among the mountains, where no man would disturb him until the end of Time. Guarding his body were the machines which had served him in life and which, Alvin knew, would never leave him now. Locked to his mind, they would wait here for the commands that could never come, until the mountains themselves had crumbled away.

The little four-legged animal which had once served man with the same devotion had been extinct too long for the boys ever to have heard of it.

They walked in silence back to the waiting ship, and presently the fortress was once more a dark lake among the hills. But Alvin did nothing to check the machine: still they rose until the whole of Lys lay spread beneath them, a great green island in an orange sea. Never before had Alvin been so high: when finally they came to rest the whole crescent of the Earth was visible below. Lys was very small now, only a dark shadow against the grey and orange of the desert—but far around the curve of the globe something was glittering like a many-colored jewel. And thus for the first time Theon saw the city of Diaspar.

They sat for a long time watching the Earth turn beneath them. Of all Man's ancient powers this surely was the one he could least afford to lose. Alvin wished he could show the world as he saw it now to the rulers of Lys and Diaspar.

"Theon," he said at last, "do you think that what I'm doing is right?"

The question surprised Theon, who as yet knew nothing of the sudden doubts that sometimes overwhelmed his friend. Nor was it easy to answer dispassionately: like Rorden, though with less cause, Theon felt that his own character was becoming submerged. He was being sucked helplessly into the vortex which Alvin left behind him on his way through life.

"I believe you are right," Theon answered slowly. "Our two peoples have been separated for long enough." That, he thought, was true, though he knew that his own feelings must bias his reply. But Alvin was still worried.

"There's one problem I haven't thought about until now," he continued in a troubled voice, "and that's the difference in our life-spans." He said no more, but each knew what the other was thinking.

"I've been worrying about that a good deal," Theon admitted, "but I think the problem will solve itself when our people get to know each other again. We can't both be right—our lives may be too short and yours are certainly too long. In time there will be a compromise."

Alvin wondered. That way, it was true, lay the only hope, but the ages of transition would be hard indeed. He remembered again those bitter words of Seranis: *"We shall both be dead when you are still a boy."* Very well: he would accept the conditions. Even in Diaspar all friendships lay under the same shadow: whether it was a hundred or a million years away made little difference at the end. The welfare of the race demanded the mingling of the two cultures: in such a cause individual happiness was unimportant. For a moment Alvin saw humanity as something more than the living background of his own life, and he accepted without flinching the unhappiness his choice must one day bring. They never spoke of it again.

Beneath them the world continued on its endless turning. Sensing his friend's mood, Theon said nothing, and presently Alvin broke the silence again.

"When I first left Diaspar," he said, "I did not know what I hoped to find. Lys would have satisfied me once—but now everything on Earth seems so small and unimportant. Each discovery I've made has raised bigger questions and now I'll never be content until I know who the Master was and why he came to Earth. If I ever learn that, then I suppose I'll start to worry about the Great Ones and the Invaders—and so it will go on."

Theon had never seen Alvin in so thoughtful a mood and did not wish to interrupt his soliloquy. He had learnt a great deal about his friend in the last few minutes.

"The robot told me," Alvin continued, "that this machine can reach the Seven Suns in less than half a day. Do you think I should go?"

"Do you think I could stop you?" Theon replied quietly.

Alvin smiled.

"That's no answer," he said, "even if it's true. We don't know what's out there in space. The Invaders may have left the Universe, but there may be other intelligences unfriendly to Man."

"Why should there be?" Theon asked. "That's one of

the questions our philosophers have been debating for ages. A truly intelligent race is not likely to be unfriendly."

"But the Invaders—?"

Theon pointed to the unending deserts below.

"Once we had an Empire. What have we now that they would covet?"

Alvin was a little surprised at this novel point of view.

"Do all your people think like this?"

"Only a minority. The average person doesn't worry about it, but would probably say that if the Invaders really wanted to destroy Earth they'd have done it ages ago. Only a few people, like Mother, are still afraid of them."

"Things are very different in Diaspar," Alvin said. "My people are great cowards. But it's unfortunate about your Mother—do you think she would stop you coming with me?"

"She most certainly would," Theon replied with emphasis. That Alvin had taken his own assent for granted he scarcely noticed.

Alvin thought for a moment.

"By now she'll have heard about this ship and will know what I intend to do. We mustn't return to Airlee."

"No: that wouldn't be safe. But I have a better plan."

The little village in which they landed was only a dozen miles from Airlee, but Alvin was surprised to see how greatly it differed in architecture and setting. The houses were several stories in height and had been built along the curve of a lake, looking out across the water. A large number of brightly colored vessels were floating at anchor along the shore: they fascinated Alvin, who had never heard of such things and wondered what they were for.

He waited in the ship while Theon went to see his friends. It was amusing to watch the consternation and amazement of the people crowding round, unaware of the fact that he was observing them from inside the machine. Theon was gone only a few minutes and had some difficulty in reaching the airlock through the inquisitive crowds. He breathed a sigh of relief as the door closed behind him.

"Mother will get the message in two or three minutes. I've not said where we're going, but she'll guess quickly enough. And I've got some news that will interest you."

"What is it?"

"The Central Council is going to hold talks with Diaspar."

"What!"

"It's perfectly true, though the announcement hasn't been made yet. That sort of thing can't be kept secret."

Alvin could appreciate this: he never understood how *anything* was ever kept secret in Lys.

"What are they discussing?"

"Probably ways in which they can stop us leaving. That's why I came back in a hurry."

Alvin smiled a little ruefully.

"So you think that fear may have succeeded where logic and persuasion failed?"

"Quite likely, though you made a real impression on the councillors last night. They were talking for a long time after you went to sleep."

Whatever the cause of this move, Alvin felt very pleased. Diaspar and Lys had both been slow to react, but events were now moving swiftly to their climax. That the climax might have unpleasant consequences for him Alvin did not greatly mind.

They were very high when he gave the robot its final instructions. The ship had come almost to rest, and the Earth was perhaps a thousand miles below, nearly filling the sky. It looked very uninviting: Alvin wondered how many ships in the past had hovered here for a little while and then continued on their way.

There was an appreciable pause, as if the robot was checking controls and circuits that had not been used for geological ages. Then came a very faint sound, the first that Alvin had ever heard from the machine. It was a tiny humming, which soared swiftly octave by octave until it was lost at the edge of hearing. There was no sense of change or motion, but suddenly he noticed that the stars were drifting across the screen. The Earth reappeared, and rolled past—then appeared again, in a slightly different position. The ship was "hunting," swinging in space like a compass needle seeking the north. For minutes the skies turned and twisted around them, until at last the ship came to rest, a giant projectile aimed at the stars.

Centered in the screen the great ring of the Seven Suns lay in its rainbow-hued beauty. A little of Earth was still visible as a dark crescent edged with the gold and crimson of the sunset. Something was happening now, Alvin knew, beyond all his experience. He waited, gripping his seat, while the seconds drifted by and the Seven Suns glittered on the screen.

There was no sound, only a sudden wrench that seemed to blur the vision—but Earth had vanished as if a giant hand had whipped it away. They were alone in space, alone with the stars and a strangely shrunken sun. Earth was gone as though it had never been.

Again came that wrench, and with it now the faintest murmur of sound, as if for the first time the generators were exerting some appreciable fraction of their power. Yet for a moment it seemed that nothing had happened: then Alvin realized that the sun itself was gone and that the stars were creeping slowly past the ship. He looked back for an instant and saw—nothing. All the heavens behind had vanished utterly, obliterated by a hemisphere of night. Even as he watched, he could see the stars plunge into it, to disappear like sparks falling upon water. The ship was travelling far faster than light, and Alvin knew

that the familiar space of Earth and Sun held him no
more.

When that sudden, vertiginous wrench came for the
third time, his heart almost stopped beating. The strange
blurring of vision was unmistakable now: for a moment,
his surroundings seemed distorted out of recognition. The
meaning of that distortion came to him in a flash of insight he could not explain. *It was real, and no delusion of
his eyes.* Somehow he was catching, as he passed through
the thin film of the present, a glimpse of the changes that
were occurring in the space around him.

At the same instant the murmur of the generators rose
to a roar that shook the ship—a sound doubly impressive,
for it was the first cry of protest that Alvin had ever heard
from a machine. Then it was all over, and the sudden
silence seemed to ring in his ears. The great generators
had done their work: they would not be needed again
until the end of the voyage. The stars ahead flared blue-
white and vanished into the ultraviolet. Yet by some
magic of Science or Nature the Seven Suns were still
visible, though now their positions and colors were subtly
changed. The ship was hurtling towards them along a
tunnel of darkness, beyond the boundaries of space and
time, at a velocity too enormous for the mind to contem-
plate.

It was hard to believe that they had now been flung out
of the Solar System at a speed which unless it were
checked would soon take them through the heart of the
Galaxy and into the greater emptiness beyond. Neither
Alvin nor Theon could conceive the real immensity of
their journey: the great sagas of exploration had completely changed Man's outlook towards the Universe, and
even now, millions of centuries later, the ancient tradi-
tions had not wholly died. There had once been a ship,
legend whispered, that had circumnavigated the Cosmos
between the rising and the setting of the sun. The billions

of miles between the stars meant nothing before such speeds. To Alvin this voyage was very little greater, and perhaps less dangerous, than his first journey to Lys.

It was Theon who voiced both their thoughts as the Seven Suns slowly brightened ahead.

"Alvin," he remarked, "that formation can't possibly be natural."

The other nodded.

"I've thought that for years, but it still seems fantastic."

"The system may not have been built by Man," agreed Theon, "but intelligence must have created it. Nature could never have formed that perfect circle of stars, one for each of the primary colors, all equally brilliant. And there's nothing else in the visible Universe like the Central Sun."

"Why should such a thing have been made, then?"

"Oh, I can think of many reasons. Perhaps it's a signal, so that any strange ship entering the Universe will know where to look for life. Perhaps it marks the center of galactic administration. Or perhaps—and somehow I feel that this is the real explanation—it's simply the greatest of all works of art. But it's foolish to speculate now. In a little while we'll know the truth."

So they waited, lost in their own dreams, while hour by hour the Seven Suns drifted apart until they had filled that strange tunnel of night in which the ship was riding. Then, one by one, the six outer stars vanished at the brink of darkness and at last only the Central Sun was left. Though it could no longer be fully in their space, it still shone with the pearly light that marked it out from all other stars. Minute by minute its brilliance increased, until presently it was no longer a point but a tiny disc. And now the disc was beginning to expand before them—

There was the briefest of warnings: for a moment a deep, bell-like note vibrated through the room. Alvin clenched the arms of his chair, though it was a futile enough gesture.

Once again the great generators exploded into life, and with an abruptness that was almost blinding, the stars reappeared. The ship had dropped back into space, back into the Universe of suns and planets, the natural world where nothing could move more swiftly than light.

They were already within the system of the Seven Suns, for the great ring of colored globes now dominated the sky. And what a sky it was! All the stars they had known, all the familiar constellations, had gone. The Milky Way was no longer a faint band of mist far to one side of the heavens: they were now at the center of creation, and its great circle divided the Universe in twain.

The ship was still moving very swiftly towards the Central Sun, and the six remaining stars of the system were colored beacons ranged around the sky. Not far from the nearest of them were the tiny sparks of circling planets, worlds that must have been of enormous size to be visible over such a distance. It was a sight grander than anything Nature had ever built, and Alvin knew that Theon had been correct. This superb symmetry was a deliberate challenge to the stars scattered aimlessly around it.

The cause of the Central Sun's nacreous light was now clearly visible. The great star, surely one of the most brilliant in the whole Universe, was shrouded in an envelope of gas which softened its radiation and gave it its characteristic color. The surrounding nebula could be seen only indirectly, and it was twisted into strange shapes that eluded the eye. But it was there, and the longer one stared the more extensive it seemed to be.

Alvin wondered where the robot was taking them. Was it following some ancient memory, or were there guiding signals in the space around them? He had left their destination entirely to the machine, and presently he noticed the pale spark of light towards which they were travelling. It was almost lost in the glare of the Central Sun, and around it were the yet fainter gleams of other worlds. Their enormous journey was coming to its end.

The planet was now only a few million miles away, a beautiful sphere of multicolored light. There could be no darkness anywhere upon its surface, for as it turned beneath the Central Sun, the other stars would march one by one across its skies. Alvin now saw very clearly the meaning of the Master's dying words: "It is lovely to watch the colored shadows on the planets of eternal light."

Now they were so close that they could see continents and oceans and a faint haze of atmosphere. Yet there was something puzzling about its markings, and presently they realized that the divisions between land and water were curiously regular. This planet's continents were not

as Nature had left them—but how small a task the shaping
of a world must have been to those who built its suns!

"Those aren't oceans at all!" Theon exclaimed suddenly.
"Look—you can see markings in them!"

Not until the planet was nearer could Alvin see clearly
what his friend meant. Then he noticed faint bands and
lines along the continental borders, well inside what he
had taken to be the limits of the sea. The sight filled him
with a sudden doubt, for he knew too well the meaning
of those lines. He had seen them once before in the desert
beyond Diaspar, and they told him that his journey had
been in vain.

"This planet is as dry as Earth," he said dully. "Its water
has all gone—those markings are the salt-beds where the
seas have evaporated."

"They would never have let that happen," replied
Theon. "I think that, after all, we are too late."

His disappointment was so bitter that Alvin did not
trust himself to speak again but stared silently at the great
world ahead. With impressive slowness the planet turned
beneath the ship, and its surface rose majestically to meet
them. Now they could see buildings—minute white in-
crustations everywhere save on the ocean beds themselves.

Once this world had been the center of the Universe.
Now it was still, the air was empty and on the ground
were none of the scurrying dots that spoke of life. Yet
the ship was still sliding purposefully over the frozen
sea of stone—a sea which here and there had gathered
itself into great waves that challenged the sky.

Presently the ship came to rest, as if the robot had at
last traced its memories to their source. Below them was
a column of snow-white stone springing from the center
of an immense marble amphitheater. Alvin waited for a
little while: then, as the machine remained motionless,
he directed it to land at the foot of the pillar.

Even until now, Alvin had half hoped to find life on this planet. That hope vanished instantly as he left the airlock. Never before in his life, even in the desolation of Shalmirane, had he been in utter silence. On Earth there was always the murmur of voices, the stir of living creatures, or the sighing of the wind. Here were none of these, nor ever would be again.

Why the machine had brought them to this place there was no way of telling, but Alvin knew that the choice made little difference. The great column of white stone was perhaps twenty times the height of a man, and was set in a circle of metal slightly raised above the level of the plain. It was featureless and of its purpose there was no hint. They might guess, but they would never know, that it had once marked the zero point of all astronomical measurements.

So this, thought Alvin sadly, was the end of all his searching. He knew that it would be useless to visit the other worlds of the Seven Suns. Even if there was still intelligence in the Universe, where could he seek it now? He had seen the stars scattered like dust across the heavens, and he knew that what was left of Time was not enough to explore them all.

Suddenly a feeling of loneliness and oppression such as he had never before experienced seemed to overwhelm him. He could understand now the fear of Diaspar for the great spaces of the Universe, the terror that had made his people gather in the little microcosm of their city. It was hard to admit that, after all, they had been right.

He turned to Theon for support, but Theon was standing, hands tightly clenched, with his brow furrowed and a glazed look in his eyes.

"What's the matter?" Alvin asked in alarm.

Theon was still staring into nothingness as he replied.

"There's something coming. I think we'd better go back to the ship."

The galaxy had turned many times upon its axis since consciousness first came to Vanamonde. He could recall little of those first eons and the creatures who had tended him then—but he could remember still his desolation when they had gone at last and left him alone among the stars. Down the ages since, he had wandered from sun to sun, slowly evolving and increasing his powers. Once he had dreamed of finding again those who had attended his birth, and though the dream had faded now, it had never wholly died.

On countless worlds he had found the wreckage that life had left behind, but intelligence he had discovered only once—and from the Black Sun he had fled in terror. Yet the Universe was very large, and the search had scarcely begun.

Far away though it was in space and time, the great burst of power from the heart of the Galaxy beckoned to Vanamonde across the light-years. It was utterly unlike the radiation of the stars, and it had appeared in his field of consciousness as suddenly as a meteor trail across a cloudless sky. He moved towards it, to the latest moment of its existence, sloughing from him in the way he knew the dead, unchanging pattern of the past.

He knew this place, for he had been here before. It had been lifeless then, but now it held intelligence. The long metal shape lying upon the plain he could not understand, for it was as strange to him as almost all the things of the physical world. Around it still clung the aura of power that had drawn him across the Universe, but that was of no interest to him now. Carefully, with the delicate nervousness of a wild beast half poised for flight, he reached out towards the two minds he had discovered.

And then he knew that his long search was ended.

How unthinkable, Rorden thought, this meeting would have seemed only a few days ago. Although he was still technically under a cloud, his presence was so obviously essential that no one had suggested excluding him. The six visitors sat facing the Council, flanked on either side by the co-opted members such as himself. This meant that he could not see their faces, but the expressions opposite were sufficiently instructive.

There was no doubt that Alvin had been right, and the Council was slowly realizing the unpalatable truth. *The delegates from Lys could think almost twice as quickly as the finest minds in Diaspar.* Nor was that their only advantage, for they also showed an extraordinary degree of coordination which Rorden guessed must be due to their telepathic powers. He wondered if they were reading the councillors' thoughts, but decided that they would not have broken the solemn assurance without which this meeting would have been impossible.

Rorden did not think that much progress had been made: for that matter, he did not see how it could be. Alvin had gone into space, and nothing could alter that. The Council, which had not yet fully accepted Lys, still seemed incapable of realizing what had happened. But it was clearly frightened, and so were most of the visitors. Rorden himself was not as terrified as he had expected: his fears were still there, but he had faced them at last. Something of Alvin's own recklessness—or was it courage?—had changed his outlook and given him new horizons.

The President's question caught him unawares but he recovered himself quickly.

"I think," he said, "it's sheer chance that this situation never arose before. There was nothing we could have done to stop it, for events were always ahead of us." Everyone knew that by "events" he meant Alvin, but there were no comments. "It's futile to bicker about the past: Diaspar and Lys have both made mistakes. When Alvin returns, you may prevent him leaving Earth again—if you can. I don't think you will succeed, for he may have learnt a great deal by then. But if what you fear has happened, there's nothing any of us can do about it. Earth is helpless—as she has been for millions of centuries."

Rorden paused and glanced along the table. His words had pleased no one, nor had he expected them to do so.

"Yet I don't see why we should be so alarmed. Earth is in no greater danger now than she has always been. Why should two boys in a single small ship bring the wrath of the Invaders down upon us again? If we'll be honest with ourselves, we must admit that the Invaders could have destroyed our world ages ago."

There was a shocked silence. This was heresy—but Rorden was interested to notice that two of the visitors seemed to approve.

The President interrupted, frowning heavily.

"Is there not a legend that the Invaders spared Earth itself only on condition that Man never went into space again? And have we not now broken those conditions?"

"Once I too believed that," said Rorden. "We accept many things without question, and this is one of them. But my machines know nothing of legend, only of truth—and there is no historical record of such an agreement. I am convinced that anything so important would have been permanently recorded, as many lesser matters have been."

Alvin, he thought, would have been proud of him now.

It was strange that he should be defending the boy's ideas, when if Alvin himself had been present he might well have been attacking them. One at least of his dreams had come true: the relationship between Lys and Diaspar was still unstable, but it was a beginning. Where, he wondered, was Alvin now?

Alvin had seen or heard nothing, but he did not stop to argue. Only when the airlock had closed behind them did he turn to his friend.

"What was it?" he asked a little breathlessly.

"I don't know: it was something terrific. I think it's still watching us."

"Shall we leave?"

"No: I was frightened at first, but I don't think it will harm us. It seems simply—interested."

Alvin was about to reply when he was suddenly overwhelmed by a sensation unlike any he had ever known before. A warm, tingling glow seemed to spread through his body: it lasted only a few seconds, but when it was gone he was no longer Alvin of Loronei. Something was sharing his brain, overlapping it as one circle may partly cover another. He was conscious, also, of Theon's mind close at hand, equally entangled in whatever creature had descended upon them. The sensation was strange rather than unpleasant, and it gave Alvin his first glimpse of true telepathy—the power which in his race had so degenerated that it could now be used only to control machines.

Alvin had rebelled at once when Seranis had tried to dominate his mind, but he did not struggle against this intrusion. It would have been useless, and he knew that this intelligence, whatever it might be, was not unfriendly. He relaxed completely, accepting without resistance the fact that an infinitely greater intelligence than his own was exploring his mind. But in that belief, he was not wholly right.

One of these minds, Vanamonde saw at once, was more sympathetic and accessible than the other. He could tell that both were filled with wonder at his presence, and that surprised him greatly. It was hard to believe that they could have forgotten: forgetfulness, like mortality, was beyond the comprehension of Vanamonde.

Communication was very difficult: many of the thought-images in their minds were so strange that he could hardly recognize them. He was puzzled and a little frightened by the recurrent fear-pattern of the Invaders; it reminded him of his own emotions when the Black Sun first came into his field of knowledge.

But they knew nothing of the Black Sun, and now their own questions were beginning to form in his mind.

"What are you?"

He gave the only reply he could.

"I am Vanamonde."

There came a pause (how long the pattern of their thoughts took to form!) and then the question was repeated. They had not understood: that was strange, for surely their kind had given him his name for it to be among the memories of his birth. Those memories were very few, and they began strangely at a single point in time, but they were crystal-clear.

Again their tiny thoughts struggled up into his consciousness.

"Who were the Great Ones—are you one of them yourself?"

He did not know: they could scarcely believe him, and their disappointment came sharp and clear across the abyss separating their minds from his. But they were patient and he was glad to help them, for their quest was the same as his and they gave him the first companionship he had ever known.

As long as he lived, Alvin did not believe he would ever again undergo so strange an experience as this soundless conversation. It was hard to believe that he could be little more than a spectator, for he did not care to admit, even to himself, that Theon's mind was so much more powerful than his own. He could only wait and wonder, half dazed by the torrent of thought just beyond the limits of his understanding.

Presently Theon, rather pale and strained, broke off the contact and turned to his friend.

"Alvin," he said, his voice very tired, "there's something strange here. I don't understand it at all."

The news did a little to restore Alvin's self-esteem, and his face must have shown his feelings, for Theon gave a sudden, not unsympathetic laugh.

"I can't discover what this—Vanamonde—is," he continued. "It's a creature of tremendous knowledge, but it seems to have very little intelligence. Of course," he added, "Its mind may be of such a different order that we can't understand it—yet somehow I don't believe that is the right explanation."

"Well, what *have* you learned?" asked Alvin with some impatience. "Does it know anything about this place?"

Theon's mind still seemed very far away.

"This city was built by many races, including our own," he said absently. "It can give me facts like that, but it doesn't seem to understand their meaning. I believe it's conscious of the past, without being able to interpret it. Everything that's ever happened seems jumbled together in its mind."

He paused thoughtfully for a moment: then his face lightened.

"There's only one thing to do: somehow or other, we must get Vanamonde to Earth so that our philosophers can study him."

"Would that be safe?" asked Alvin.

"Yes," answered Theon, thinking how uncharacteristic his friend's remark was. "Vanamonde is friendly. More than that, in fact—he seems almost affectionate."

And quite suddenly the thought that all the while had been hovering at the edge of Alvin's consciousness came clearly into view. He remembered Krif and the small animals that were constantly escaping ("It won't happen again, Mother") to annoy Seranis. And he recalled—how long ago that seemed!—the zoological purpose behind their expedition to Shalmirane.

Theon had found a new pet.

They landed at noon in the glade of Airlee, with no thought of concealment now. Alvin wondered if ever in human history any ship had brought such a cargo to Earth—if indeed Vanamonde was located in the physical space of the machine. There had been no sign of him on the voyage: Theon believed, and his knowledge was more direct, that only Vanamonde's sphere of attention could be said to have any location in space.

As they left the ship the doors closed softly behind them and a sudden wind tugged at their clothes. Then the machine was only a silver dot falling into the sky, returning to the world where it belonged until Alvin should need it again.

Seranis was waiting for them as Theon had known and Alvin had half expected. She looked at the boys in silence for a while, then said quietly to Alvin:

"You're making life rather complicated for us, aren't you?"

There was no rancor in the words, only a half-humourous resignation and even a dawning approval.

Alvin sensed her meaning at once.

"Then Vanamonde's arrived?"

"Yes, hours ago. Since dawn we have learned more of history than we knew existed."

Alvin looked at her in amazement. Then he understood: it was not hard to imagine what the impact of Vanamonde must have been upon this people, with their keen perceptions and their wonderfully interlocking minds. They had reacted with surprising speed, and he had a sudden incongruous picture of Vanamonde, perhaps a little frightened, surrounded by the eager intellects of Lys.

"Have you discovered what he is?" Alvin asked.

"Yes. That was simple, though we still don't know his origin. He's a pure mentality and his knowledge seems to be unlimited. But he's childish, and I mean that quite literally."

"Of course!" cried Theon. "I should have guessed!"

Alvin looked puzzled and Seranis took pity on him.

"I mean that although Vanamonde has a colossal, perhaps an infinite, mind, he's immature and undeveloped. His actual intelligence is less than that of a human being"—she smiled a little wryly—"though his thought processes are much faster and he learns very quickly. He also has some powers we do not yet understand. The whole of the past seems open to his mind, in a way that's difficult to describe. He must have used that ability to follow your path back to Earth."

Alvin stood in silence, for once somewhat overcome. He realized how right Theon had been to bring Vanamonde to Lys. And he knew how lucky he had been ever to outwit Seranis: that was not something he would do twice in a lifetime.

"Do you mean," he asked, "that Vanamonde has only just been born?"

"By his standards, yes. His actual age is very great, though apparently less than Man's. The extraordinary thing is that he insists that *we* created him, and there's no doubt that his origin is bound up with all the great mysteries of the past."

"What's happening to Vanamonde now?" asked Theon in a slightly possessive voice.

"The historians of Grevarn are questioning him. They are trying to map out the main outlines of the past, but the work will take years. Vanamonde can describe the past in perfect detail, but since he doesn't understand what he sees it's very difficult to work with him."

Alvin wondered how Seranis knew all this: then he realized that probably every waking mind in Lys was watching the progress of the great research.

"Rorden should be here," he said, coming to a sudden decision. "I'm going to Diaspar to fetch him."

"*And* Jeserac," he added, in a determined afterthought.

Rorden had never seen a whirlwind, but if one had hit him the experience would have felt perfectly familiar. There were times when his sense of reality ceased to function, and the feeling that everything was a dream became almost overwhelming. This was such a moment now.

He closed his eyes and tried to recall the familiar room in Diaspar which had once been both a part of his personality and a barrier against the outer world. What would he have thought, he wondered, could he have looked into the future when he had first met Alvin and seen the outcome of that encounter? But of one thing he was sure and a little proud: he would not have turned aside.

The boat was moving slowly across the lake with a gentle rocking motion that Rorden found rather pleasant. Why the village of Grevarn had been built on an island he could not imagine: it seemed a most inconvenient arrangement. It was true that the colored houses, which seemed to float at anchor upon the tiny waves, made a scene of almost unreal beauty. That was all very well, thought Rorden, but one couldn't spend the whole of one's life staring at scenery. Then he remembered that this was precisely what many of these eccentric people did.

Eccentric or not, they had minds he could respect. To him the thoughts of Vanamonde were as meaningless as a thousand voices shouting together in some vast, echoing cave. Yet the men of Lys could disentangle them, could record them to be analyzed at leisure. Already the structure of the past, which had once seemed lost forever, was becoming faintly visible. And it was so strange and unexpected that it appeared to bear no resemblance at all to the history that Rorden had always believed.

In a few months he would present his first report to Diaspar. Though its contents were still uncertain, he knew that it would end forever the sterile isolation of his race. The barriers between Lys and Diaspar would vanish when their origin was understood, and the mingling of the two great cultures would invigorate mankind for ages to come. Yes even this now seemed no more than a minor by-product of the great research that was just beginning. If what Vanamonde had hinted was indeed true, Man's horizons must soon embrace not merely the Earth, but must enfold the stars and reach out to the Galaxies beyond. But of these further vistas it was still too early to be sure.

Calitrax, chief historian of Lys, met them at the little jetty. He was a tall, slightly stooping man, and Rorden wondered how, without the help of the Master Associators, he had ever managed to learn so much in his short life. It did not occur to him that the very absence of such machines was the reason for the wonderful memories he had met in Grevarn.

They walked together beside one of the innumerable canals that made life in the village so hazardous to strangers. Calitrax seemed a little preoccupied, and Rorden knew that part of his mind was still with Vanamonde.

"Have you settled your date-fixing procedure yet?" asked Rorden presently, feeling somewhat neglected.

Calitrax remembered his duties as host and broke contact with obvious reluctance.

"Yes," he said. "It had to be the astronomical method.

We think it's accurate to ten thousand years, even back to the Dawn Ages. It could be even better, but that's good enough to mark out the main epochs."

"What about the Invaders? Has Bensor located them?"

"No: he made one attempt but it's hopeless to look for any isolated period. What we're doing now is to go back to the beginning of history and then take cross-sections at regular intervals. We'll link them together by guesswork until we can fill in the details. If only Vanamonde could interpret what he sees! As it is we have to work through masses of irrelevant material."

"I wonder what he thinks about the whole affair: it must all be rather puzzling to him."

"Yes, I suppose it must. But he's very docile and friendly, and I think he's happy, if one can use that word. So Theon believes, and they seem to have a curious sort of affinity. Ah, here's Bensor with the latest ten million years of history. I'll leave you in his hands."

The Council chamber had altered little since Alvin's last visit, for the seldom-used projection equipment was so inconspicuous that one could easily have overlooked it. There were two empty chairs along the great table: one, he knew, was Jeserac's. But though he was in Lys, Jeserac would be watching this meeting, as would almost all the world.

If Rorden recalled their last appearance in this room, he did not care to mention it. But the councillors certainly remembered, as Alvin could tell by the ambiguous glances he received. He wondered what they would be thinking when they had heard Rorden's story. Already, in a few months, the present had changed out of all recognition—and now they were going to lose the past.

Rorden began to speak. The great ways of Diaspar would be empty of traffic: the city would be hushed as Alvin had known it only once before in his life. It was waiting, waiting for the veil of the past to be lifted again after—if Calitrax was right—more than fifteen hundred million years.

Very briefly, Rorden ran through the accepted history of the race—the history that both Diaspar and Lys had always believed beyond question. He spoke of the unknown peoples of the Dawn Civilizations, who had left behind them nothing but a handful of great names and the fading legends of the Empire. Even at the beginning, so the story went, Man had desired the stars and at last attained them. For millions of years he had expanded across the Galaxy, gathering system after system beneath his sway. Then, out of the darkness beyond the rim of the universe, the Invaders had struck and wrenched from him all that he had won.

The retreat to the Solar System had been bitter and must have lasted many ages. Earth itself was barely saved by the fabulous battles that raged round Shalmirane. When all was over, Man was left with only his memories and the world on which he had been born.

Rorden paused: he looked round the great room and smiled slightly as his eyes met Alvin's.

"So much for the tales we have believed since our records began. I must tell you now that they are false— false in every detail—*so false that even now we have not fully reconciled them with the truth.*"

He waited for the full meaning of his words to strike home. Then, speaking slowly and carefully, but after the first few minutes never consulting his notes, he gave the city the knowledge that had been won from the mind of Vanamonde.

It was not even true that Man had reached the stars. The whole of his little empire was bounded by the orbit of Persephone, for interstellar space proved a barrier beyond his power to cross. His entire civilization was huddled round the sun, and was still very young when—the stars reached him.

The impact must have been shattering. Despite his failures, Man had never doubted that one day he would conquer the deeps of space. He believed too that if the Universe held his equals, it did not hold his superiors. Now he knew that both beliefs were wrong, and that out among the stars were minds far greater than his own. For many centuries, first in the ships of other races and later in machines built with borrowed knowledge, Man had explored the Galaxy. Everywhere he found cultures he could understand but could not match, and here and there he encountered minds which would soon have passed altogether beyond his comprehension.

The shock was tremendous, but it proved the making of the race. Sadder and infinitely wiser, Man had returned to the Solar System to brood upon the knowledge he had gained. He would accept the challenge, and slowly he evolved a plan which gave hope for the future.

Once, the physical sciences had been Man's greatest interest. Now he turned even more fiercely to genetics and the study of the mind. Whatever the cost, he would drive himself to the limits of his evolution.

The great experiment had consumed the entire energies of the race for millions of years. All that striving, all that sacrifice and toil, became only a handful of words in Rorden's narrative. It had brought Man his greatest victories. He had banished disease: he could live forever if he wished, and in mastering telepathy he had bent the most subtle of all powers to his will.

He was ready to go out again, relying upon his own resources, into the great spaces of the Galaxy. He would meet as an equal the races of the worlds from which he had once turned aside. And he would play his full part in the story of the Universe.

These things he did. From this age, perhaps the most

spacious in all history, came the legends of the Empire. It had been an Empire of many races, but this had been forgotten in the drama, too tremendous for tragedy, in which it had come to its end.

The Empire had lasted for at least a billion years. It must have known many crises, perhaps even wars, but all these were lost in the sweep of great races moving together towards maturity.

"We can be proud," continued Rorden, "of the part our ancestors played in this story. Even when they had reached their cultural plateau, they lost none of their initiative. We deal now with conjecture rather than proven fact, but it seems certain that the experiments which were at once the Empire's downfall and its crowning glory were inspired and directed by Man.

"The philosophy underlying these experiments appears to have been this. Contact with other species had shown Man how profoundly a race's world-picture depended upon its physical body and the sense organs with which it was equipped. It was argued that a true picture of the Universe could be attained, if at all, only by a mind which was free from such physical limitations—a pure mentality, in fact. This idea was common among most very ancient religions and was believed by many to be the goal of evolution.

"Largely as a result of the experience gained in his own regeneration, Man suggested that the creation of such beings should be attempted. It was the greatest challenge ever thrown out to intelligence in the Universe, and after centuries of debate it was accepted. All the races of the Galaxy joined together in its fulfilment.

"Half a billion years were to separate the dream from the reality. Civilizations were to rise and fall, again and yet again the age-long toil of worlds was to be lost, but the goal was never forgotten. One day we may know the full story of this, the greatest sustained effort in all history. Today we only know that its ending was a disaster that almost wrecked the Galaxy.

"Into this period Vanamonde's mind refuses to go. There is a narrow region of time which is blocked to him; but only, we believe, by his own fears. At its beginning we can see the Empire at the summit of its glory, taut with the expectation of coming success. At its end, only a few thousand years later, the Empire is shattered and the stars themselves are dimmed as though drained of their power. Over the Galaxy hangs a pall of fear, a fear with which is linked the name "the Mad Mind."

"What must have happened in that short period is not hard to guess. The pure mentality had been created, but it was either insane or, as seems more likely from other sources, was implacably hostile to matter. For centuries it ravaged the Universe until brought under control by forces of which we cannot guess. Whatever weapon the Empire used in its extremity squandered the resources of the stars: from the memories of that conflict spring some, though not all, of the legends of the Invaders. But of this I shall presently say more.

"The Mad Mind could not be destroyed, for it was immortal. It was driven to the edge of the Galaxy and there imprisoned in a way we do not understand. Its prison was a strange artificial star known as the Black Sun, and there it remains to this day. When the Black Sun dies, it will be free again. How far in the future that day lies there is no way of telling."

Alvin glanced quickly around the great room, which had become utterly silent. The councillors, for the most part, sat rigid in their seats, staring at Rorden with a trancelike immobility. Even to Alvin, who had already heard the story in fragments, Rorden's narrative still had the excitement of a newly unfolding drama. To the councillors, the impact of his revelations must be overwhelming.

Rorden was speaking again in a quiet, more subdued voice as he described the last days of the Empire. This was the age, Alvin had decided, in which he would have liked to live. There had been adventure then, and a superb and dauntless courage—the courage that can snatch victory from the teeth of disaster.

"Though the Galaxy had been laid waste by the Mad Mind, the resources of the Empire were still enormous, and its spirit was unbroken. With a courage at which we can only marvel, the great experiment was resumed and a search made for the flaw that had caused the catastrophe. There were now, of course, many who opposed the work and predicted further disasters, but they were overruled. The project went ahead and, with the knowledge so bitterly gained, this time it succeeded.

"The new race that was born had a potential intellect that could not even be measured. But it was completely infantile: we do not know if this was expected by its creators, but it seems likely that they knew it to be inevitable. Millions of years would be needed before it reached maturity, and nothing could be done to hasten the process. Vanamonde was the first of these minds: there must be others elsewhere in the Galaxy, but we believe that only a very few were created, for Vanamonde has never encountered any of his fellows.

"The creation of the pure mentalities was the greatest achievement of Galactic civilization: in it Man played a major and perhaps a dominant part. I have made no reference to Earth itself, for its story is too small a thread to be traced in the great tapestry. Since it had always been drained of its most adventurous spirits our planet had inevitably become somewhat conservative, and in the end it opposed the scientists who created Vanamonde. Certainly it played no part at all in the final act.

"The work of the Empire was now finished: the men of that age looked round at the stars they had ravaged in their desperate peril, and they made the decision that might have been expected. They would leave the Universe to Vanamonde.

"The choice was not hard to make, for the Empire had now made the first contacts with a very great and very strange civilization far around the curve of the Cosmos. This civilization, if the hints we can gather are correct, had evolved on the purely physical plane further than had been believed possible. There were, it seemed, more solutions than one to the problem of ultimate intelligence. But this we can only guess: all we know for certain is that within a very short period of time our ancestors and their fellow races have gone upon a journey which we cannot follow. Vanamonde's thoughts seem bounded by the confines of the Galaxy, but through his mind we have watched the beginning of that great adventure—"

A pale wraith of its former glory, the slowly turning wheel of the Galaxy hangs in nothingness. Throughout its length are the great empty rents which the Mad Mind has torn—wounds that in ages to come the drifting stars will fill. But they will never restore the splendor that has gone.

Man is about to leave his Universe, as once he left his world. And not only Man, but the thousand other races that have worked with him to make the Empire. They have gathered together, here at the edge of the Galaxy, with its whole thickness between them and the goal they will not reach for ages.

The long line of fire strikes across the Universe, leaping from star to star. In a moment of time a thousand suns have died, feeding their energies to the dim and monstrous shape that has torn along the axis of the Galaxy and is now receding into the abyss. . . .

"The Empire had now left the Universe, to meet its destiny elsewhere. When its heirs, the pure mentalities, have reached their full stature we believe it will return again. But that day must still lie far ahead.

"This, in its outlines, is the story of Galactic civilization. Our own history, which we thought so important, is no more than a belated episode which we have not yet examined in detail. But it seems that many of the older, less adventurous races refused to leave their homes. Our direct ancestors were among them. Most of these races fell into decadence and are now extinct: our own world barely escaped the same fate. In the Transition Centuries—which really lasted for millions of years—the knowledge of the past was lost or else deliberately destroyed. The latter seems more probable: we believe that Man sank into a superstitious barbarism during which he distorted history to remove his sense of impotence and failure. The legend of the Invaders is certainly false, and the Battle of Shalmirane is a myth. True, Shalmirane exists, and was one of the greatest weapons ever forged— but it was used against no intelligent enemy. Once the Earth had a single giant satellite, the Moon. When it began to fall, Shalmirane was built to destroy it. Around that destruction have been woven the legends you all know, and there are many such."

Rorden paused, and smiled a little ruefully.

"There are other paradoxes that have not yet been resolved, but the problem is one for the psychologist rather than the historian. Even my records cannot be wholly trusted, and bear clear evidence of tampering in the very remote past.

"Only Diaspar and Lys survived the period of decadence—Diaspar thanks to the perfection of its machines, Lys owing to its partial isolation and the unusual intellectual powers of its people. But both cultures, even when they had struggled back to their former level, were distorted by the fears and myths they had inherited.

"Those fears need haunt us no longer. All down the ages, we have now discovered, there were men who rebelled against them and maintained a tenuous link between Diaspar and Lys. Now the last barriers can be swept aside and our two races can move together into the future—whatever it may bring."

"I wonder what Yarlan Zey would think of this?" said Rorden thoughtfully. "I doubt if he would approve."

The Park had changed considerably, so far very much for the worse. But when the rubble had been cleared away, the road to Lys would be open for all to follow.

"I don't know," Alvin replied. "Though he closed the moving ways, he didn't destroy them as he might very well have done. One day we must discover the whole story behind the Park—and behind Alaine of Lyndar."

"I'm afraid these things will have to wait," said Rorden, "until more important problems have been settled. In any case, I can picture Alaine's mind rather well: once we must have had a good deal in common."

They walked in silence for a few hundred yards, fol-

lowing the edge of the great excavation. The Tomb of
Yarlan Zey was now poised on the brink of a chasm, at
the bottom of which scores of robots were working furi-
ously.

"By the way," said Alvin abruptly, "did you know that
Jeserac is staying in Lys? Jeserac, of all people! He likes
it there and won't come back. Of course, that will leave a
vacancy on the Council."

"So it will," replied Rorden, as if he had never given
the matter any thought. A short time ago he could have
imagined very few things more unlikely than a seat on the
Council; now it was probably only a matter of time.
There would, he reflected, be a good many other resigna-
tions in the near future. Several of the older councillors
had found themselves unable to face the new problems
pouring upon them.

They were now moving up the slope to the Tomb,
through the long avenue of eternal trees. At its end, the
avenue was blocked by Alvin's ship, looking strangely
out of place in these familiar surroundings.

"There," said Rorden suddenly, "is the greatest mystery of all. *Who was the Master?* Where did he get this
ship and the three robots?"

"I've been thinking about that," answered Theon. "We
know that he came from the Seven Suns, and there might
have been a fairly high culture there when civilization on
Earth was at its lowest. The ship itself is obviously the
work of the Empire.

"I believe that the Master was escaping from his own
people. Perhaps he had ideas with which they didn't
agree: he was a philosopher, and a rather remarkable
one. He found our ancestors friendly but superstitious
and tried to educate them, but they misunderstood and
distorted his teachings. The Great Ones were no more
than the men of the Empire—only it wasn't Earth they
had left, but the Universe itself. The Master's disciples

didn't understand or didn't believe this, and all their mythology and ritual was founded on that false premise. One day I intend to go into the Master's history and find why he tried to conceal his past. I think it will be a very interesting story."

"We've a good deal to thank him for," said Rorden as they entered the ship. "Without him we would never have learned the truth about the past."

"I'm not so sure," said Alvin. "Sooner or later Vanamonde would have discovered us. And I believe there may be other ships hidden on Earth: one day I mean to find them."

The city was now too distant to be recognized as the work of Man, and the curve of the planet was becoming visible. In a little while they could see the line of twilight, thousands of miles away on its never-ending march across the desert. Above and around were the stars, still brilliant for all the glory they had lost.

For a long time Rorden stared at the desolate panorama he had never seen before. He felt a sudden contemptuous anger for the men of the past who had let Earth's beauty die through their own neglect. If one of Alvin's dreams came true, and the great transmutation plants still existed, it would not be many centuries before the oceans rolled again.

There was so much to do in the years ahead. Rorden knew that he stood between two ages: around him he could feel the pulse of mankind beginning to quicken again. There were great problems to be faced, and Diaspar would face them. The recharting of the past would take centuries, but when it was finished Man would have recovered all that he had lost. And always now in the background would be the great enigma of Vanamonde—

If Calitrax was right, Vanamonde had already evolved more swiftly than his creators had expected, and the philosophers of Lys had great hopes of future co-operation which they would confide to no one. They had become very attached to the childlike supermind, and perhaps they believed that they could foreshorten the eons which his natural evolution would require. But Rorden knew that the ultimate destiny of Vanamonde was something in which Man would play no part. He had dreamed, and he believed the dream was true, that at the end of the Universe Vanamonde and the Mad Mind must meet each other among the corpses of the stars.

Alvin broke into his reverie and Rorden turned from the screen.

"I wanted you to see this," said Alvin quietly. "It may be many centuries before you have another chance."

"You're not leaving Earth?"

"No: even if there are other civilizations in this Galaxy, I doubt if they'd be worth the trouble of finding. And there is so much to do here—"

Alvin looked down at the great deserts, but his eyes saw instead the waters that would be sweeping over them a thousand years from now. Man had rediscovered his world, and he would make it beautiful while he remained upon it. And after that—

"I am going to send this ship out of the Galaxy, to follow the Empire wherever it has gone. The search may take ages, but the robot will never tire. One day our cousins will receive my message, and they'll know that we are waiting for them here on Earth. They will return, and I hope that by then we'll be worthy of them, however great they have become."

Alvin fell silent, staring into the future he had shaped but which he might never see. While Man was rebuilding his world, this ship would be crossing the darkness between the galaxies, and in thousands of years to come it would return. Perhaps he would be there to meet it, but if not, he was well content.

They were now above the Pole, and the planet beneath them was an almost perfect hemisphere. Looking down upon the belt of twilight, Alvin realized that he was seeing at one instant both sunrise and sunset on opposite sides of the world. The symbolism was so perfect and so striking that he was to remember this moment all his life.

In this Universe the night was falling: the shadows were lengthening towards an east that would not know another dawn. But elsewhere the stars were still young and the light of morning lingered: and along the path he once had followed, Man would one day go again.